PERFECT MATCH: THE THIEF WHO LOVED ME

PERFECT MATCH SERIES

I. T. LUCAS

1

MARCUS/WILLIAM

William opened his eyes to a glaring sunlight and the feeling of sand tickling his toes. He blinked, his mind momentarily blurry—what had he been doing just now?

"William? Will, are you there?" The frantic voice sounded in his ear.

He shook off his brief malaise and lifted his hand to the low-profile earpiece he was wearing. "I'm right here. Stop fretting, Liam."

He pretended to scratch his head and lowered his hand. Reaching for the earpiece had been a rookie move, and his moment of fugue was inexcusable.

His handler back at the agency snorted. "Worrying about you is my job, Will. Now, down to business. Do you have the *Evening Star* in your sights?"

Casually lifting his cell phone, William scanned the boats in the harbor. The tracking technology installed on the device instantly honed in on the preprogrammed identifying markers, magnified them, and correlated them to the information in the harbor's database—which William had hacked into earlier.

"She's here," he said after a minute. "She's going by the *Pearl* right now, but physical characteristics are a ninety-five percent match."

"Excellent. You know what to do…"

"Of course. Get on board, plant the bug, and get off without anyone any the wiser."

"Exactly. And fast, if you don't mind. We've got a situation developing here at headquarters that you're getting pulled into. The sooner you get back, the better."

"I've hardly had a chance to enjoy the Seychelles." He stood up, stared at his phone, and then looked around the harbor like a clueless tourist. "It's lovely here this time of year, quite balmy. It would do you some good to get out of your cubicle and into the sunshine once in a while."

William wasn't eager to go back to the dreary headquarters and the somber faces occupying it, including his handler's.

"We have sunshine in England," Liam replied. "Perhaps not as much of it as you are enjoying out there, but it suits me just fine. Now less chatter, more getting a move on."

"Ruthless taskmaster," William muttered as he moved.

His oversized, colorful shirt-and-shorts combo provided plenty of room for the Glock 19 he'd tucked into the small of his back. Getting the weapon into the remote tropical country had been a challenge even for a seasoned operative like him, but it was worth the trouble. He could have gotten a weapon locally, but his aim was best with his own handgun, which was like an extension of his hand. Naturally, he also had two knives on him, not to mention the garrote imitating a handwoven leather bracelet on his left wrist, but those were just accessories, the icing on the cake, so to speak.

William ambled along, staring at his phone and then glancing up in seeming befuddlement every few feet or so. It was the work of a moment to identify the boat's security personnel. One man was stationed on the dock in front of it, and two men were up on the boat itself. None of them were the notorious captain of the *Evening Star*, but they also weren't the average dockhands. Their shoulders were too broad, bulked up by the jackets they wore, even in the heat of the island, to hide their weapons.

Honestly, if they were trying to fit in, they were doing a poor job of it.

How to get past them, though? He couldn't put the bug just anywhere. Inside was best. Outside would do in a pinch, but it had to be well away from the waterline. Besides, it would be far too visible against the pristine white hull.

Hmm...

He stumbled along the dock leading to the yacht, shielding his eyes as if he was nursing a hangover and keeping his face down while looking at the phone.

Twenty feet...fifteen...

"Hey!"

Oh, English, excellent.

"Ah, hello?" William pretended to startle as he looked up from his phone. The man loomed over him, which didn't happen often. At six foot two, he rarely had to look up at anyone's face. "Yeah, right. Are you the glass-bottom boat people?"

The man's stern expression faltered into confusion. "What?"

"The boat, the glass bottom...Look, the missus wants to see the fishes, right? And if I don't make it happen, I'll be sleeping with them, so I booked a ride for us today. This is the right dock, innit?"

William watched the bull-like man heave a heavy breath and let it out slowly through his flared nostrils. "This isn't the boat you're looking for."

William laughed. "You a *Star Wars* fan, mate? Is this part of your patter? Love it!" He laughed heartily and slapped the man on the shoulder. "But seriously, this is it, right? Bloody thing's called the *Black Pearl*, God only knows why given how white this thing is, so...hang on, lemme on board, and I'll text my wife to come join us."

"You!" Bull Man lost the little cool he had and lunged for William, clearly intent on moving him forcibly away from the yacht.

William jerked back at the last second, put his foot out just so, and—

Splash.

Bull Man tripped over William's leg, and arms careening, fell into the muddy brown water.

"Oof, bad place for swimming, mate!" William called after him as he made his way up the gangplank.

Holding the phone in one hand, he palmed the bug he'd placed in his pocket with the other. It was matte black and the size of a dime. All he needed was to find a good place to stick it.

"What the hell?" one of the other men barked as he caught sight of William. He stalked over, his gait purposeful, smooth and even.

William needed to move away fast.

"You the drinks guy? I'll have a martini, thanks," he said quickly before ducking into the cabin.

Unlike the deck, which was fairly spartan, this part of the yacht was sumptuous with burnished wood and metal fittings, leather furniture, an enormous flatscreen TV, and a well-equipped bar. It was also devoid of people, although William could hear a woman's laughter from downstairs.

He needed to work fast.

Ducking down in front of the couch, he pressed the bug in place on the underside of the leather—black, which was perfect.

Then he tossed his phone a few feet away and yelled, "Shite!"

The man who'd been running him down outside entered the cabin just in time to see William crawl over to his phone and pick it up. "I dropped the bloody thi—whoa!" William went limp in the man's grasp as he was half-dragged, half-carried over to the door and back into the unrelenting sunshine.

"Who the hell are you?" the man demanded.

"I'm here for the boat tour!" William insisted. "I bought a boat tour on the *Black Pearl*! This is it, yeah, mate?"

"No," the man replied grimly. "Wrong boat. Mate." He

glanced over at the other man on deck. "What should we do with him?"

"Don't bother the boss with a fuckup like this," the other man said disinterestedly. "Shoot him and throw him over the side."

"Oh, hey now." William raised his hands placatingly. "There's no need for violence, guys, c'mon. Harmless misunderstanding, yeah? Look, I'll just be on my way, no problem at all, let me—"

"You're dead!" The shout came from the very wet, angrier-than-ever Bull Man who'd just run up the gangplank.

Without waiting for acknowledgment, he thundered toward William with a look that promised far worse than dying of a bullet to the head.

Too bad he wasn't going to live out his hopes and dreams today. William smirked as he twisted the arm of the man who was holding him, turning his wrist up and over so that he not only let go of William's collar, he had to stumble around in a wide, awkward pivot.

It just so happened that his sideways momentum met Bull Man's forward energy, sending them both crashing down to the deck in a tangle of limbs and curses.

William was on the third man before he could finish pulling out his gun, striking him hard in the throat with the flat of his hand to bend him over and following it up with a knee to the face. He would have done more, but one of the other two idiots had gotten a gun out. A bullet crashed into the gunwale, and William decided it was time to leave.

He ran for the gangplank, tossing a two-fingered salute behind him along with a cry of, "Piss off, you wankers!"

There were a few more gunshots, but William was well away by the time the men guarding the place had sorted themselves out.

"Please tell me that during all of that, you managed to plant the bloody bug," Liam growled in his ear.

"Of course I did," William scoffed as he headed for his car. "Do you take me for an amateur?"

He'd rented a little Kia Rio for this mission, one of hundreds like it. He'd have preferred a Porsche, but maintaining a low profile had been crucial for the job.

Actually, there was a lovely-looking Maserati right over there…

No, nope. Mind on the job, no time for hot-wiring pretty cars.

It was time to sail off into the sunset—literally. The Seamax M-22 he had stashed at a private slip on the other side of the island would get him to the Maldives, and from there, he'd fly back to London.

As William started the rental and pulled out of the lot, he saw the three brutes he'd tangled with making themselves obnoxious to the harbor master.

Excellent timing.

"How's that situation you mentioned earlier?" he asked Liam as he headed for the road that would take him around the island.

It was a beautiful day, trees swaying in the breeze, the scents of a dozen different tropical fruits mingling with the sea air.

It was calm, placid. Peaceful.

Boring.

"Developing rather quickly," Liam replied. "Get back here as soon as you can."

Grinning, William pressed on the gas and zoomed past a slow passenger van on a blind turn. Surprisingly, the little car had oomph to it. Perhaps he'd have some fun with the Rio before returning it to the rental place.

"I'm on it."

2

MARIAN/CLAUDETTE

A single light shone through the darkness as Claudette ducked down behind the solar panel array on the top of Clarence House, agilely dodging the roaming torch of the property's night guard, who was making his thirty-minute pass around the perimeter of the enormous structure.

He ought to be moving on in three…two…

The light passed around the far corner of the property, and Claudette breathed a sigh of relief. It wasn't that she'd been worried about the guard, but attempting what she was about to do, she couldn't afford to let even the slightest thing put her at a disadvantage.

Every move had to be executed perfectly tonight, every step forward crystal clear and precise. After all, she'd been planning this job for months now, and having all that effort go to waste because a rent-a-cop got lucky with his torch would be embarrassing.

Not that it would.

This job would go flawlessly.

It had to.

Soon, the Honeycomb Tiara would be moved from this less heavily-guarded location, and getting into Buckingham Palace would be a lot harder than getting into the royals' secondary home in London.

Creeping along the roof, Claudette silently made her way over to the skylight. She knelt down by the glass and got out her laser-cutting apparatus. She attached it to the large pane closest to the roof and began cutting out a half-circle that would be just big enough to fit her body through.

Slow, slow...

She couldn't rush this step.

Dropping the cut section would be disastrous.

When she got within an inch, she slowed even further, cutting with one hand while stabilizing the window with the other. Finally, it came free, and she lifted the glass up and out and set it aside.

The laser cutter went back into her bag, and the infrared lights came out. These high-intensity beams had done the trick of overwhelming the motion detectors she'd practiced on back home.

For the past five years, Claudette had tried it with every make and model, and they'd worked each time beautifully. They would get the job done here as well. The tricky part was to hit the actual detectors, which was complicated since she couldn't duck her head down to look at them.

That, of course, was what cameras were for.

The infrared lights were attached to a slender telescoping pole, the end of which also sported a ring of cameras that would send a composite picture to her phone, so that she knew exactly when she'd made contact with the detectors. The close end of the rod attached with a suction cup to the skylight, so once it was set with the lights on, the security system in this room would be effectively disabled.

It took several minutes to get things in place, and then a few waves of her extended hand down into the room verified that the detectors were, in fact, blocked.

Perfect.

She grinned behind her mask as she got into position, then slowly lowered herself down.

Slowly...slowly...no sense in rushing it.

All those hours of Pilates came in handy now, not to mention the time she spent on the climbing wall.

Lower, lower...

Fully extended, Claudette was only about five feet from the floor. Perfect. Now to—

Crack!

The edge of the skylight suddenly fractured.

She lost her right-hand grip, and it flew backward—right into her infrared light setup.

Shite.

She had three seconds to recover—that was the grace period most motion detectors had after being blocked—or she'd be face to face with a whole host of guards in another ten.

In less than three seconds, Claudette dropped to the floor, caught her gear in one hand, then rolled behind the nearest chair, which luckily was huge and Victorian. One of the detectors gave a warning chirp but thankfully subsided before breaking into a full-blown alarm.

To think that she had almost been done in by the bloody architecture. Claudette rolled her eyes and got to work slowly, painstakingly setting up her lights to block the detectors again. It took five minutes she couldn't afford to spare, but eventually, it was done.

She stood up in the fourth floor's largest meeting room and sighed in relief. Now, to get to the bedroom where she had been told the tiara was being kept.

She'd gotten intel from one of the maids, which had been a risky move but necessary.

Usually she didn't involve anyone in her jobs, but given that this place had five bedrooms to pick from and seemed to be in a constant state of renovation, getting inside intelligence had seemed prudent. Claudette had paid the woman handsomely enough to afford the lovely vacation the maid was currently on.

Hopefully, her intel was reliable.

Using a third infrared torch, Claudette slowly made her way from the meeting room down the hall, blocking the motion detectors and darting forward in a stop-start, stop-start motion that threatened to bore her to death. Taking out the entire alarm system would have made this part much easier, but it would have also been much riskier.

This was the proper way to do it, despite how she loathed the snail's pace. On and on she went until she finally made it to the royals' bedroom.

Away went the light, out came the lock picks.

For all that the property had been modernized, some things were apparently too historically important to get rid of, and the doors fell into that category. Claudette had the old-school skeleton keyhole lock open in under five seconds, and with one last glance down the hall, she slipped inside the room.

Finally, she could relax a little.

The royal family didn't allow any surveillance equipment in their most private space, so once she was this far in, she didn't have to worry about motion detectors, cameras, or a roaming guard.

Perfect.

Claudette pulled her full-face mask off, running one hand through her long ponytail before finally scratching the itch on her nose that had been bothering her since she fell from the edge of the roof. She grinned, then tucked her lock picks away and looked around. She didn't turn on the light. There was no need to draw attention to the room, even if it wasn't being actively surveilled. She could do her searching in the dark.

It wouldn't take long.

No one would expect a burglar in Clarence House, of all places.

She let herself relax as she wandered around the room, enjoying the ambiance of the place while she was searching for the tiara. She was no stranger to the luxuries that wealth could bring. As an heiress to a substantial fortune, she'd grown up surrounded by the best, but there was something about this place that seemed so homey. Nothing like the grandeur of Buckingham Palace, or the cool elegance of

Kensington Palace, this place felt like somewhere people could actually live rather than perform.

She shook her head. *Get your head out of the clouds.*

It was time to wrap this up. The Honeycomb Tiara had to be here somewhere.

Claudette began by opening drawers and looking inside the wardrobes, then she checked the roll-top desk and the nightstands. By the time she'd been through the closet, she was starting to get concerned. It was supposed to be there.

It had to be there.

She'd paid a quarter of a million bloody pounds to ensure the thing was in this room at this time, and so help her, if she'd been played...

Look for a safe.

Of course. This might be a personal residence, but protecting the Crown Jewels was practically in the job descriptions of the royals. Naturally, they would be in a safe.

That was fine. Claudette had brought everything she needed to crack the most likely models. Gently knocking on the walls, she found no hidden safes there, and there was nothing under the floor either.

Perhaps it was hidden behind the curtains by the bed.

She walked over and began pulling back the thick brocade curtain, which was gathered at the right side of the bed, and froze.

Feet!

Those were feet she'd just revealed.

Shit!

Claudette spun around and ran.

3

MARCUS/WILLIAM

Now, this is more like it!

Fighting back a grin, William gave chase after the limber sprite.

To say that he'd been irritated when he'd been told about his next assignment would be a massive understatement, but now that he'd gotten a glimpse of her, he decided that it was worth the trouble after all.

He'd gone from fighting goons on the backside of a tropical paradise, to flying a plane for way too long, to being on another plane for even longer, only to get less than four hours of sleep before being given his new task by Liam—to lie in wait for a thief and catch her in the act of attempting to burgle Clarence House.

How prosaic for one of the top members of His Majesty's Secret Service.

Surely there was a better use for him than that.

His complaints had been met with stoicism from his handler. "The bosses have plans for the thief in question," he'd said, the neon lights reflecting unpleasantly off his balding pate. It had been almost bright enough to make William wince. Did Liam polish it up on purpose? "Your job is to apprehend her without injuring her and without making a scene. Do you understand?"

"If you're so certain she's responsible for everything you say she is, why not just go and arrest her now?"

"Because she's the best at what she does," Liam had replied bluntly. "Not a trace of evidence left behind, no witnesses, nothing. We've been building a circumstantial case against Claudette Roth for years, but if it weren't for the testimony of a maid she bribed, we wouldn't even know about this attempt at the Crown Jewels."

Claudette Roth. William knew a bit about her from reading the red-tops' headlines.

Heiress to the Roth fortune, one of the aristocracy-adjacent set who mingled with the landed gentry all while finagling to become one of them.

He had little patience for people like that, people who'd gotten what they had due to the work of people long generations ago—so long ago that many of their descendants had forgotten what actual work was. They floated through life concerned with trivialities and maintaining their fortunes and status.

"Why on earth would a woman with that pedigree turn to thievery?"

"Who knows?" Liam had shrugged. "Perhaps she started down the path because she was bored. From all accounts, she's highly intelligent. She has a business degree from Oxford."

"Half the idiots in Parliament have degrees from Oxford, but that doesn't make them smart."

"Regardless, you're on detail. We assume the heist is going to happen tonight, so I want you in Clarence House before the last of the staff checks out for the day. Here's the name of your contact." He'd handed over a business card. "You'll have the usual getup allotted to you, as needed. Remember, though—no guns."

"What if she pulls a gun on me?"

"Then take it away from her. Or is a hundred-and-twenty-pound woman going to prove too much for you?"

"Ha-bloody-ha." William had a hard time imagining a society woman who could get the better of him like that. Oh, he'd had his arse kicked in training by several ladies, but they were professionals, some of the most capable and dangerous people in the business. Claudette Roth was a well-heeled tart looking to get her kicks at the expense of royalty, and for his part, William would have preferred to see her get away with it.

The headlines would be fantastic.

But that wasn't his job, and he wouldn't balk just because he found a particular assignment beneath him.

He'd gone through the motions of preparation—getting a keycard, speaking with the man in charge of the staff, planning the best spot for him to lie in wait, etc.

Once the lights were out, he'd settled into a meditative state, one that left him ready to move but didn't require him to be on edge.

Perhaps he'd sunk a bit too deep into that state—it

wasn't until he heard the rattle of the lock being breached that he cottoned on to the fact that she was here.

Roth had actually made it this far without setting off an alarm. Good for her. Now he could apprehend her in person.

He waited with careful stillness behind the heavy curtain at the side of the bed.

Soon...soon...

As soon as she stopped admiring herself in the bloody mirrors or whatever was taking her so long.

Honest to God, why wasn't she—

And then she was. He had one moment to take in her face, unexpectedly lovely in person even when her eyes were the size of saucers, and then the chase was on.

William had expected to be able to run her down easily. He hadn't expected to need to leap over the chairs, vases, and other household furnishings she flung into his path.

She was quick, he would give her that, both mentally and physically.

She reached the meeting room a full three seconds ahead of him, and he just barely missed catching her heel as she leaped off the arm of a heavy Victorian chair, grabbed the hole in the skylight she'd made, and hauled herself up and out without pause.

Roth stopped there, looking down at him with a fierce expression on her face. "Don't come after me," she warned, then pulled a balaclava over her face and took off.

Like hell, he wasn't going after her. William gauged the distance and leaped up to the edge of the skylight—

Which immediately fell apart beneath his hands, sending

him crashing down onto his back. In the distance, he thought he heard a woman's laugh.

"Will?" That was Liam finally checking in. "What's going on?"

"Roth's in the wind," he snapped as he got to his feet. "Managed to get ahead of me."

He looked around feverishly, searching for anything that might work to enlarge the hole above him.

Ah. Hopefully, the king wouldn't begrudge him using a bust of his namesake like this. He hurtled the statue at the skylight, which shattered nicely, then grabbed the chair and pulled it over into the wreckage. "I'm going after her."

"What the bloody hell was that noise?"

"A bit of structural damage, nothing that can't be fixed," William assured Liam as he stepped onto the chair and reached over the rotting edge of the skylight to the stone beyond it. It was an awkward lift, but he managed it.

"Nothing that can't be fixed? That's one of the residences of the king and queen, you tosser!"

William tapped the earpiece twice, his way of telling Liam to shut up, please, things were getting serious now, then looked around.

Where would she have...ah. He ran for the side of Clarence House that adjoined St. James's Palace, and sure enough, there was the dark silhouette of a woman at the far edge of the palace itself. She moved very fast. There was no way he'd catch up to her now if he took her route. Better to climb down here and run around on the ground.

Fortunately, there were all sorts of handholds to be had on this very classic architecture. William made his way to the ground in under twenty seconds and sprinted toward Friary Court.

Please don't divert, please don't divert, please don't divert...

If she'd chosen to double back or take a less direct route down, he'd almost certainly lose Roth at this point. He was the only agent assigned to the task of bringing her in, largely because he'd insisted.

Wouldn't that be ironic? To fail because he was allergic to teamwork?

William made it to Friary Court just as a familiar dark-garbed figure leaped over the wrought iron fence.

"Hey! Stop!" he called out.

She froze for a second as she saw him, then raced toward the Mall and beyond to St. James's Park. Perhaps she thought she'd lose him in the trees.

Not bloody likely.

William put on a burst of speed, cutting the distance between them in half by the time they reached the sward. "Stop!" he called out again. "Don't make this any harder for your—oof!"

He barely managed to dodge the equipment she threw at him, some sort of camera attachment.

Goodness, she was pulling out all the stops. It was only fair to her that he do the same.

"Stop, or I'll shoot!" he yelled.

Immediately, Roth slowed to a jog, then to a stop. Chest heaving, breath coming in short gasps, she turned around with her hands—well, not up, but at least on her hips so he could see that she wasn't going for a gun of her own.

"Who the hell do you think you are?" she snapped, voice

clearly irate even behind her mask. "This is London, not the Wild West! You can't just go threatening to shoot people!"

Ah, so she retained a touch of naïveté after all. How cute. "You can when you're a member of MI6," William replied, taking some satisfaction in how her eyes widened briefly. "And in point of fact," he added as he closed the last of the distance between them, "I only threatened to shoot you. I couldn't actually have done it, darling. I'm not carrying a gun."

"I'll—" Roth immediately lashed out with a punch, swift enough that William couldn't dodge it, just turned enough to take it on the side of the head rather than the face. "Show you a—" She punched him again, this time in the gut, bending him over. "Darling!" Her knee came up, ready to knock him in the head and likely knock him out. A classic pattern.

Unfortunately for her, it was one that William knew well. He blocked her incoming knee with both arms, jabbing the top of her thigh with his elbow as he did.

She shrieked, falling back as the pain of the knot he'd just introduced to her muscles sank in.

Staying low, he cut in close and got her in an ankle pick, sending her straight down onto her back.

She didn't stay there for more than a split second, though, moving smoothly into a roll and getting back onto her feet.

"Bloody—" William had to duck again as she chucked another camera at him. "Look, I'm here to offer you a deal, not to arrest you. We have a job we need you for. You're just making it worse for yourself by resisting!"

"Am I? Because I already know you're not going to shoot me," she rejoined saucily. "And I'm not going to be made into some sort of government drone. Look, let me go, and I'll leave England and never come back."

"Come with me, and I'll make sure your involvement with the government ends after a single contract," he promised.

"Um, Will." That was Liam in his ear. "You actually don't have the authority to make that promise—"

Roth laughed. "You clearly don't have the authority to make that decision," she said, the sneer evident in her voice. "You're a foot soldier, nothing more. MI6, maybe, but low-level. Who's pulling your strings, little puppet?"

Little puppet? She deserved a good spanking just for that.

The thievery would require a sterner punishment, like going through MI6 training. That would teach her some humility.

"What's motivating you to steal, little thief?" he taunted. "What makes a beautiful, wealthy woman like yourself branch out into something as petty as swiping gems from royals who'll barely notice they're gone? Are you an adrenaline junkie? Or maybe you're funding a less savory addiction with it?" He grinned and cocked his head. "Or perhaps it's just that Daddy didn't hug you enough when you were a—"

The punch caught him just below his right eye, sending his head snapping back. William reeled, barely managing to keep on his feet.

Roth stalked toward him, anger in every line of her

body. "Don't you ever talk about my father, do you understand? I will—"

"Oi! What's going on over there?"

Immediately, Roth's whole demeanor changed. She ripped the mask off her face, stuffed it into the pouch she was wearing, then threw the entire lot of it into the lake behind them.

"Help!" she called out with perfectly mimed frenzy as she quickly pulled the collar of her top down over her shoulders and folded up the sleeves. It left her looking less like a thief in the night and more like a modestly dressed young woman. "Please help!" She thrust a finger toward William. "Officer, this man attacked me!"

"What?" William gaped. "Are you bloody kidding me?"

The officer got to them a few seconds later, torch in one hand, baton out in the other. "What's that?" He looked from Roth to William and back again. "You say he attacked you?"

"He did!" Her eyes welled up with crocodile tears. "He's been following me for almost six streets, and I told him to go away, but he just didn't listen to me, and…and…." The officer turned a dark look on William, and Roth took advantage of the shift in his attention to shoot William a triumphant smile.

"I've got people headed your way to handle this," Liam said in his ear. "Just don't let her walk away."

Well, then. She wanted to play the damsel in distress card? William could work with that.

"Me attack you?" he said incredulously. "Are you mad? Look at this!" He pointed at his eye, which was stinging like the devil and swelling up. "Look at what she did to me, and for no reason! She led me all the way out here, promised me a good time—then clocked me in the face! I think she's tryin' to rob me, mate."

Roth went from self-satisfied to indignant in a second. "That's ridiculous," she exclaimed.

"Is it? Then why'd you throw your bag of stuff away as soon as the police got close, eh?" He turned to the policeman. "Do a little mucking in the edge of the lake, and you'll find it. She just threw it in a minute ago." There. Now he had hard facts on his side.

"Come now, how could I do something like that to him?" Roth twisted one lock of hair around her finger in an endearingly nervous way. "He's twice my size! Please, just let me go, I—"

"Ah, Miss, I can't do that." The officer shook his head. "If you're serious about 'im attackin' you, then you'll need to press charges. Can't do that 'ere. And if you're serious about her trying to rob you?" he said to William. "Same thing. Both of you come down to the station with me, and we'll get this sorted out."

"I'm already running quite late for an appointment," Roth said apologetically, raising her voice a bit to be heard over the distant sound of a helicopter. "I won't press charges if he won't, but I'd truly appreciate you keeping him here with you for a few moments so that I can get a bit of a head start. I don't trust him not to follow me."

Given the minute changes in her posture, Roth was about to run again, and William readied himself to go after her, and for the policeman to subsequently come after him.

Getting arrested was not how he'd pictured this night going. This would be a delight to explain to the authorities.

Before either of them could move, the helicopter he'd been idly tracking suddenly swooped in right above them, its floodlight so bright it was nearly blinding.

Roth and the police officer both winced and shaded their eyes.

"No one make any sudden movements," an augmented voice shouted down at them. "Officer, that woman is a threat to national security. Agent Kentworth, secure Miss Roth immediately."

"With pleasure," William said, pulling cuffs out of his inside jacket pocket.

Roth stared at him dumbfounded as he put on the restraints, but that stare soon gave way to a glare.

"This isn't over," she said, the ironclad promise of it reflected in both her voice and those bright hazel-brown eyes.

Even as tired and battered as he was, William had to admit she was one of the most beautiful women he'd ever seen. It was as if fate had reached into his mind, plucked out his ideal of female beauty, and given it flesh.

The attraction wasn't only about her looks, though. It was just as much about her impudent spunk and intelligence.

He smiled his most charming smile. "I certainly hope not, darling."

4

MARIAN

One month earlier

"What a bastard!" Gigi dissolved into tears. "I can't believe he would do this to me. I gave him twenty-two years of my life, and he—"

Handing her client another tissue, Marian kept her face in a well-practiced expression of nonjudgmental compassion and friendliness.

It wasn't that she didn't feel genuinely sorry for the woman, but Marian was a highly-paid professional, and her job wasn't to be Gigi's friend. Her job was to get her the best possible divorce settlement.

Like many of her clients, Gigi Webb was attractive, intelligent, and highly accomplished, but her life was falling apart because she was married to the wrong man.

After two decades together, he had decided that his wife

and the life they'd built together were less important than screwing his intern. He hadn't even been careful about hiding the affair. It was as if he wanted his wife to find out.

"At least you have your boys," Marian said gently.

"They are the only good to come from that jackass," Gigi said with a derisive sniff. Then her face fell. "This is so hard on them. They love their father, and finding out he's leaving us for a 'work friend' has been awful."

Oh, crap. "He's not filing for custody, is he?"

Gigi had told Marian that her husband wasn't interested in joint custody, but cheaters often used children as leverage to get better settlement terms.

"No." Gigi's eyes went perfectly still, staring off into the distance at something only she could see. "He didn't even mention the boys. Doesn't want anything coming between him and his walking, talking penis sheath."

It was hard not to crack a smile. Marian had heard cheating partners described in many different ways, but "penis sheath" was a new one.

She composed herself back to equanimity. "Maybe he'll feel differently later and decide that he wants to take part in their lives."

"He'll be lucky if I give him the chance." Gigi finally met her eyes again. "I want to make this as painful for Harry as possible, do you hear me? Whenever he thinks of me after this, I want him to remember me as the bitch who took it all and laughed while doing it."

"Gigi…"

"I'm serious." The older woman leaned in closer to her. "Peter told me you're the best. You got him full custody of his kids and have his ex paying half her salary in alimony on top of child support. I want that, but more. I want the house, I want the boat, I want his goddamn Lamborghini. Can you do that for me?" Her eyes shuttered, going cold. "You are supposed to be the best."

Marian was the best, and she had a ruthless reputation that had the attorneys for the other side shaking in their Ferragamo loafers. There was a certain satisfaction in that, but the truth was that she hated her job. So yeah, she was helping people, and she was making excellent money, but her life was mired in strife.

It wasn't very glamorous or exciting either.

Most cases got settled out of court, and the largest part of her job was writing emails and filing paperwork.

She put a professional smile on her face. "I can do all that and more. Let's get the broad strokes down on paper, and then we'll meet again next week after you've talked with your financial planner about your and Harry's joint assets."

Half an hour later, when the soon-to-be ex-Mrs. Webb was gone, Marian let out a breath. She needed a stiff drink and to kick off the high heels that were pinching her toes. Pulling out a bottle of fine Scotch from the liquor cabinet, she poured herself a finger. Usually, the bottle was reserved for when she closed a case, but the contract she'd just signed with Gigi was lucrative, and the case was one she felt good about taking on.

Harry Webb deserved to be destroyed, and she was the right attorney for the job.

Closing her eyes, Marian downed the Scotch in a single swallow.

This is why I'm never getting married. It always goes up in flames.

God, did she even know anyone who was happily married anymore?

Her parents had called it quits when she was five, her brother had been hitched for all of three months before the cracks started to show, and all of her besties from grad school were either separated or divorced.

Had her grandparents been happy together? It had seemed so, but who really knew?

From what she'd seen so far, and she'd seen a lot, marriage was nothing but a multi-layered lie, where outward happiness and prosperity covered up bleak dissatisfaction.

The days when a woman needed to be married in order to be considered a respectable member of society were long gone, and Marian was intensely grateful for that. There was still some stigma attached to being divorced, especially when children were involved, but Gigi would weather it just like Marian's other clients had.

They had no other choice. Life had to go on.

Marian laid her hand over her abdomen. Then there were people like her, who wanted to become a parent but didn't have an appropriate partner.

I've never been at a loss for partners. But appropriate ones... well, I can't even think of one.

Not the adventurous Vincente who had complimented her on her firm, flexible body, or kind and boring Frank, who'd loved doing couple massages and spa days together, or hot sex-god Ryu who'd kept her up late every night the entire month they had been dating. They were all decent men, but none were right for her, and definitely not candidates to father her children.

She would do better raising a baby on her own than tying her life to a guy she couldn't stand being around for more than a couple of weeks. Creating a child together was a bond with someone else that could never be broken.

Gigi could never wipe Harry entirely out of her life because of the two sons they shared. No thank you. If no man met Marian's requirements, she would do it without one.

She was used to doing everything on her own anyway, and the freedom of not having to depend on anyone for anything was priceless. Well, the price was loneliness, but the price for compromising her standards was misery, so there was that.

Setting her glass down, Marian returned to her desk and pressed the call button. "Lila? What does the rest of the day look like?"

"One sec, boss." A moment later, her secretary opened the door and strode into the room.

As usual Lila was impeccably dressed, and her hair was pulled up in an elegant chignon, but her porcelain-doll-like appearance was misleading. The woman had the meanest right hook Marian had ever seen—better than a professional bodyguard at keeping angry spouses out of the office.

"Let's see." Lila peered at her tablet. "You've got a meeting with Reggie's lawyer at three to review a few points in the settlement they're balking at."

"Is he still harping on about the private jet?" Marian

interjected irritably. "He knows he's got to sell it. It's the only fiscally viable course for him to take."

Lila rolled her eyes. "Word on the grapevine is that he's courting a bunch of new investors, trying to get their buy-in and a fresh cash infusion to prop him up."

If he was under the illusion that he could shield assets from the divorce settlement, he was in for a rude awakening. Marian had an excellent team of private investigators and forensic accountants at her disposal, and with the fees she was being paid, she wasn't afraid to use them.

Her barracuda reputation was well-earned.

"Anything he gets before the divorce is finalized is fair game for his wife to lay claim to as well."

"It's just hearsay," her secretary said, "but I'm betting it's solid."

Marian pursed her lips. "Reggie is just the sort of guy to try to hide assets. Get Hank on it."

The private investigator had a team adept at everything from following a mark to hunting down Swiss bank accounts. They'd followed a client's spouse to the Caymans once to catch her violating the terms of her alimony settlement.

"Will do." Lila looked back at the tablet in her hands. "After that, there's a mediation between the Yancys, then court for the Underwood case, and then—oh!" She practically jumped with excitement. "You're not gonna believe this, but I just got a call from Veronica Pierce."

"What?"

Why on earth would Veronica be calling them now? Her divorce had been finalized almost eight years ago. It was one of Marian's first big wins with the firm and had solidified for her the fact that marriage was a bogus institution.

"Why?"

"Apparently, she's considering a reconciliation and wants to talk about—"

"What?" It was rude to interrupt, but Marian couldn't help it. "Reconciliation? With..." What was his name again... "With Oliver? The man who gambled away their joint assets under the guise of 'risky investing' until there was nothing left of their net worth but her inheritance? Are you serious?"

Lila shrugged. "I guess she is. I mean, the message says something about the years of therapy he's gone through, and how he's being completely open with her about his struggles, all in the hopes of proving to her that he's worthy of a second chance. She seems tempted."

"Well, she needs to get un-tempted, fast."

Ridiculous. Men like Oliver Pierce never changed. Marian had squeezed him as hard as Veronica would let her, which wasn't nearly as hard as she would have liked, and had gotten her client out of a bad situation and into a whole new life. And now she was courting that disaster all over again?

Not your business, not your problem.

Except it was, because Veronica was reaching out to her to discuss the ridiculous reconciliation.

Talk about settling. Veronica could do much better than go back to her good-for-nothing ex.

"Put her off for now," Marian said tiredly. "I'll deal with her when things calm down a bit."

"So never, then," Lila said with a smirk but made the appropriate notation on the tablet. "That's it for today."

"Thanks." Marian took a deep, centering breath, then opened Reginald Davenport's file. She was going to have words with his lawyer when they met.

5

MARCUS

The alarm clock blaring at four-thirty in the morning had never sounded more baleful to Marcus than it did today. As he struggled to wake up, his eyelids felt like they'd been weighed down with sandbags. Groaning, he rolled from his back onto his stomach and pressed his face into the pillow.

Would Doug be put off if he canceled today?

Perhaps he could tell him a white lie that he was down with the flu. Or he could even tell his trainer the truth, that he'd been up until one in the morning, dealing with the date from hell.

If not for the burning scratch on his cheek, Marcus would have thought he'd had a nightmare.

Still groggy from sleep, he tried to remember how the pleasant, if bland, evening had turned into a shit show.

It had all started because of a condom.

She—Teri or Tiffany, or something like that—had thrown a tantrum of gargantuan proportions when Marcus had made it clear that he wasn't going to sleep with her without protection.

"What?" she'd shrieked from the middle of his bed as he reached toward his bedside table. "Why? I told you I'm clean. I said I'm on birth control! Don't you trust me?"

"I just met you three hours ago," Marcus had pointed out, rather reasonably, he thought.

He'd gotten a pillow to the face for his logical assessment of their involvement.

After that the date had devolved into a stand-off, with her locking herself in the bathroom and refusing to leave until he apologized for ruining her dreams and aspirations of having a loving and trusting relationship.

Reluctantly, he'd apologized just to get her out of there and be done with the drama, but when she'd opened the door and wanted to get him back in bed, sans the condom of course, he'd naturally refused and asked her to leave. That had resulted in her attacking him like a rabid animal, shrieking and scratching.

Marcus's cheek still burned where she'd clawed him.

He'd had to call building security and then his lawyer. Peter Shultz hadn't been happy to be woken up at midnight to issue a warning and get a signed NDA from the hysterical woman.

Marcus had finally fallen into bed around two, which meant he'd had an entire two and a half hours of restless sleep before the start of his morning routine.

Sleep was a siren call, but the habitual routine's pull proved stronger. He needed the workout to sweat out the negative energy coursing through his body and prepare for the high-stress day at the office. It wouldn't be the first time he'd made it through the day on just a few hours of sleep.

Hell, it wouldn't even be the first time that week.

Sticking to a regimented routine was the key to his success. Discipline, hard work, and ruthless tenacity had brought him to where he was today—one of the top hedge fund managers in the country.

Marcus rolled over and forced himself to his feet. His penthouse apartment was cool, and with the blanket gone, his skin pebbled with goosebumps. It was another effective technique to wake him up and get ready faster. As long as he could force himself out of bed, the rest of the morning usually took care of itself.

He dressed mechanically, slipping into his Gymshark workout wear before heading to the bathroom to brush his teeth and shave.

Resolute about getting this done as fast as possible, he spread shaving cream onto his skin, then pulled his jaw taut as he lifted his razor to his face.

Brushing his teeth could be done without looking in the mirror, but unfortunately, he still had to stare at himself in order to shave.

Marcus met his gaze and barely recognized the man staring back at him. Dark circles beneath his eyes dimmed the bright blue he'd inherited from his mother—the only thing he'd gotten from her. The rest of his face was almost identical to his father's, from the square jaw to the aquiline nose that had a slight bump in the middle from being broken that one time in college.

His hair was thick and dark, curled with sweat from his uneasy sleep, and there was not a single strand of grey yet.

He was as fit as the best personal trainer in all of Manhattan could get him, with defined muscles in his arms and abs, but his damn hand was shaking like it belonged to an old man.

Marcus was in the prime of his life. So why was his hand shaking, and why did he feel so goddamn old?

Screw it. Shaving could wait. He wiped his face clean with a damp towel, then headed for the kitchen to grab a bottle of the fruit-infused water his personal chef had prepared for him.

Nothing but the best for Marcus Shurman, so why the hell did he still feel so empty?

6

MARIAN

By the time Marian had made it back to her high-rise apartment, she was dead on her feet. The day had felt long, even for her, and as usual it had been filled with acrimony and deceit.

It should have been easy to simply go from dinner to shower to bed without pause, but of course—of course—it had ended up being one of those nights when her brain just wouldn't shut off.

She couldn't stop thinking about Veronica.

Reconciliation.

But why?

What was it about a man who'd cheated her out of millions that could be worth a second chance? Eventually he'd come clean, and with Marian's help, Veronica had come out of the mess with a decent parachute, still…

So yeah, he loved her, that much was clear, but he didn't love her enough not to steal in the first place.

It was true that they'd gone through a lot of life together, and divorce had clearly been Veronica's last resort, and even in the throes of the process, the fact that she'd still loved him had been evident. But she should know better. He cheated once, and he would cheat again.

People didn't change.

Surely being alone was better than being with someone you couldn't trust. It had to be better. It had to. Not everyone's marriage was miserable. Some people must have wonderful relationships. But that was so rare that Marian had lost hope of ever finding her happily ever after.

Yeah, keep telling yourself that.

She hadn't gotten to where she was today by lying to herself.

So yeah, she was a little lonely, and she hated coming home to an empty house and craved having someone waiting for her with a smile and a warm embrace. She also missed having someone to go to bed with.

Lord, when had her last date been?

Two months ago? Three? Or was it four?

When was that charity auction?

Oh, wait, she hadn't had sex with that guy. The night had ended early once she'd realized he'd never managed to speak above boob level. She was an intelligent and interesting woman, but he hadn't listened to a word she'd said.

You're spiraling. Change the song playing in your head.

It was nearly five o'clock in the morning, and if she didn't catch at least a couple hours of shuteye, she would be a walking zombie throughout the day. Fortunately, she didn't have any courtroom time scheduled, so perhaps she could catch a nap on the couch in her office between clients.

With a sigh, Marian turned on the large flatscreen TV across from her bed. This late, or rather this early in the morning, there was nothing on but reruns and infomercials, both of which tended to put her right to sleep.

Five minutes, and she would be out.

"Are you a busy professional with no time to search for your soulmate?" a warm, inviting female voice said, "or take a much-needed vacation?" The image on the screen switched from a couple walking hand in hand on the beach to the same couple white-water rafting. "Are you tired of surfing endless profiles on dating apps and going out on disappointing dates?" Several funny memes of disastrous first dates flashed across the screen. "If so, then Perfect Match Virtual Studios has the answer for you. Your dream vacation with a perfect partner is only a few keyboard clicks away. Whether you come for relaxation, adventure, or to find your soulmate, Perfect Match will custom-tailor your experience so you can live out your fantasy with the most compatible partner, safely and anonymously." A beautiful couple danced across a ballroom floor, the woman in a glittering blue ballgown, the man in a tux.

Were they even real, or were those computer-generated images?

These days, it was hard to tell. CGI had gotten so good that soon actors would no longer need to be pretty because their bodies and faces would be replaced by perfect computer-generated avatars.

"With Perfect Match, you can choose to be anyone." The

screen split in two, each side showing a gorgeous computer-generated avatar that looked entirely realistic. "Based on a very detailed questionnaire, an avatar will be generated for you, further ensuring your anonymity and enhancing your experience. At Perfect Match, you never have to worry about meeting your partner in the real world unless both of you choose to do so."

A series of avatars was shown, ranging from gorgeous to fantasy creatures and even the bizarre. Why would anyone want to live out a fantasy as a Pegasus?

"Your adventure can take place anywhere your imagination takes you." The camera panned out, showing a view of a planet on the screen that wasn't Earth.

And was that a spaceship? Intrigued, Marian sat up in bed.

The smiling spokeswoman's face filled the screen. "Perfect Match Studios guarantee the highest-quality immersive environment possible. If we don't meet and exceed your expectations, your next adventure is on us, and if we fail to satisfy you the second time, we will issue you a full refund."

The commercial ended with contact information.

'For more details, go to www.PerfectMatchVirtualFantasy.com.

Your virtual fantasy is only a few keyboard clicks away.'

Well, that sounded almost too good to be true. If she didn't enjoy the experience, she could get a refund, so why not give it a try?

But wait, did that mean partnering with a real person? Wasn't it all just virtual?

Excitement bubbling in her chest, Marian clicked the

television off, snatched her phone from the nightstand, and typed into the search bar the URL provided at the end of the commercial.

7

MARCUS

At precisely four-fifty-five, the guard from the lobby called. "Douglas McCormick is here for you, sir. Should I let him in?"

It wasn't the regular guy working the night shift. Benny would have known to let Doug in without calling. "Mr. McCormick is on the list of approved guests," Marcus said, trying not to sound exasperated. "You don't need to call me to clear him."

"Yes, sir. My mistake. I should have checked the list first. I'll buzz him in."

"No need. Mr. McCormick has the code to my private lift."

Doug was a big guy, a former Marine, and showing up at such an ungodly hour must have unsettled the new guy, especially after the fiasco with Trisha or Tiffany or whatever her name was. Nevertheless, he should have followed protocol and checked the damn list. That was why having systems and sticking to them was so important.

Letting out a breath, Marcus headed to his personal gym and began his stretching routine. Once he'd worked up a good sweat and later had his first cappuccino of the day, he'd feel human again.

"Morning, sunshine!" Douglas called as soon as he walked through the front door.

Marcus rolled his eyes. It was the same thing every morning. If they hadn't been friends since before either of them had been famous, he would have been tempted to tell Doug exactly where he could stick his sunshine.

Actually...

"Shove your sunshine," he said as Doug walked into the gym. "I dwell in darkness."

"Ooh, someone's grumpy today." Doug didn't look at him as he set down his bag, but when he straightened up and turned to face Marcus, his expression became concerned. "You weren't kidding. You do look like a creature of the night. What happened to your face?"

Marcus grimaced. "Her name was...Trisha, I think. Or Teri."

Doug nodded solemnly. "I assume that's not the result of rough sex games. Lady trouble again, Marcus?"

He laughed caustically. "Building security had to escort her out."

His friend winced. "Ouch. That's a first."

Yeah. It hadn't been one of Marcus's best moments, but it hadn't been his worst either. A couple of antacids would take care of the burning in his stomach.

"Could be worse," Marcus sighed.

Doug opened his mouth to say something, but thankfully reconsidered and got in position instead. "Let's start with stretching."

"I've already started on the calves."

"Good, then we can continue from there."

As Doug led him through his usual warm-up routine, chatting the entire time about his famous clients and the celebrity gym he was planning to open, Marcus felt the tension in his shoulders gradually abate.

Training with Douglas was a good way to start a day, not just because the guy was an excellent trainer, but also because he projected the kind of calm and joy that Marcus could only experience vicariously through his old friend.

He liked listening to Doug's exploits.

The tales of name-redacted 'but you probably know who they are' client shenanigans enlivened the early morning sessions, but today he was too tired to pay attention, focusing more on Doug's cheerful tone of voice than what the guy was actually saying.

With warm-up done, Marcus turned to the treadmill, but Doug's hand on his arm stopped him.

"No treadmill today," his trainer said, a glint in his eyes. "Your mind is not in sync with your body right now, and the last thing you need is to fly off the treadmill because you put your foot down wrong."

Marcus scowled. "Should we move on to the weights?"

"Nope." Doug grinned. "Let's spar. You need to release all that negative energy you're bottling up inside, and there is no better way to do that than to kick the shit out of someone. Not that you have a chance in hell to kick my ass, but you can try. Get your gloves."

It had been a while since they'd sparred, and it was precisely what Marcus needed. "Prepare to kiss the mat, my friend," he said as he went to get his grappling gloves.

They were thick enough to take the sting out of punches but still let him grab and hold if he tried to put on a lock. He got his mouth guard and took position in the center of the room.

"Big words from someone looking like a kid who's gotten into mom's makeup bag," Doug shot back as he turned to get his sparring gear.

Was he referring to the dark circles under his eyes? Or the red scratches on his cheek?

Waiting for Doug to step onto the mat, Marcus got in position, and as soon as his trainer did the same, he went on the offensive with a double-leg takedown.

Doug sprawled, putting all his weight on Marcus's back as he tried to slip an arm under him and roll him onto his back. Marcus got a knee up, threw a few hard punches to Doug's side to get him to let go, then reached out for an ankle pick, sending his trainer to the floor. He didn't have time to celebrate, though. A second later, Doug swept his feet out from under him.

They spent the next forty minutes sparring, Doug's MMA-style moves taking them from flat on the mat to their feet and back again. Marcus was pretty good, but Doug had passed up a career in the UFC to create his personal training business. He could have tapped Marcus ten times in as many minutes, but instead, he kept them moving, trading punches and kicks, throws and takedowns, then grappling for a while before restarting on their feet.

It was just what Marcus had needed.

When they were done, he was physically exhausted but mentally clear, and he was ready to take the day by storm.

8

MARIAN

As Marian pored over the Perfect Match website, reading every review, her resolve to try the service strengthened.

The reviewers raved about the experience, with the most common complaint being the high cost. But even the complainers said that it was worth it and that they would do it again. Some even said that the high price tag was a good thing because the experience could easily become addictive, and it should be reserved for finding a soulmate or special occasions.

Busy entrepreneurs and executives enthused about the mini-vacation element of the experience, pointing out that a real vacation would have cost much more than a virtual session in The Perfect Match Studios. The experience lasted days or weeks inside the virtual world, but in reality, it took only three hours. The time saved was even more valuable than the cost.

Marian leaned against the stack of pillows and closed her eyes.

On the face of things, it seemed like a perfect solution for her. She was a busy professional, hadn't taken a real vacation in years, and had the money to spend.

The idea of enjoying a custom-tailored adventure with someone else—a second mind to make things interesting and unexpected—was thrilling and titillating, but at the same time, and for the same reason, worrisome.

What if she got matched up with a pervert? What sorts of things could a sociopath or a narcissist get up to in an environment like that?

In her line of work, Marian had to contend with more than enough of those types, and she didn't need to deal with one in a virtual world too. That would ruin her fantasy, and the money-back guarantee was not enough to compensate her for the emotional damage an experience like that would leave.

But then, the service seemed legit. None of the reviewers had complained about their partners, and Perfect Match conducted extensive psychiatric evaluations to vet their clients. True, those evaluations were based on the comprehensive questionnaires each applicant had to fill in, and people could lie on those, but with thousands of answered questions, the doctors or the artificial intelligence they used could see past the lies.

It wasn't just something you could pay to play. That, along with the personal medical supervision during the experience, was what had sold it to Marian. There was quality control on the technology, and the founders seemed committed to making it as safe as possible for their users while still retaining the excitement of it all.

And it really did look...exciting.

She could have a daring adventure and, as a bonus, some worry-free sex. As a hint of warmth welled between her thighs, Marian glanced over at her bedside table, where the latest run of Black Cat's comics was sitting.

Given her chosen profession, it was ironic that she had always been drawn to the idea of playing a role like that—glittering and gorgeous by day, breaking and entering by night. To be clever enough to pull off heists, leave no one the wiser, and do it all with the respect and admiration of a few select friends and lovers.

The truth was that what she did for a living was rarely exciting, and once she'd achieved partner status, she didn't really have anything more to aspire to. She already had celebrity clients, was already semi-famous in attorney circles, and was already making great money. And yet she was still as restless and unsatisfied as she'd been in high school when she'd dreamt of one day becoming what she was now.

Everything in her life had worked out perfectly according to plan, and there had been no surprises along the way. Perhaps it was time to veer off the path she'd set out on and take a chance on something different.

Live a little.

Opening her eyes, Marian lifted her phone and returned to the Perfect Match home page to check their available locations. There was one in New York and another one in Los Angeles. All she needed to do to start the process was fill out a basic online application and wait for further instructions.

Fingers hovering over the keyboard, she hesitated again.

What am I afraid of?

No one will ever know.

I can have all the fun I want, no strings attached, and no hearts broken.

9

MARCUS

"Seriously," Doug said as Marcus drained his water bottle. "You need to stop with the hookups. I can't remember the last time you had a date that went well." He tilted his head. "Unless you only tell me about the bad ones and keep the good ones to yourself, you've had a very long, nasty streak."

Marcus shrugged. "Not all of them were as disastrous as this one, and I know not to expect too much from club hookups. At least it's better than dating apps. I get to see the women as they really are, not their photoshopped versions. When I make my move, I like to look a woman in the eyes and see her reaction."

The hunt was half the fun.

Prowling clubs, he felt like a hunter, and as the ladies took a gander at his good looks, his expensive clothing, and his impeccable grooming, they clamored for the opportunity of being his prey. He loved seeing the flare of desire in their eyes, the slight parting of the lips as their breath hitched, the crossing of the legs, the hardening of their nipples...

Yeah, he was a sucker for the female body, and with his brain focused on sex, it was no wonder he kept missing all the warning signs. Evidently, even a smart and capable man like him was easily rendered stupid by beautiful women.

And to think that females were considered the weaker sex.

Huh. They had all the power, and the smart ones knew how to wield it over horny men.

Douglas didn't look impressed with his speech. "Yeah, but looking them in the eyes hasn't saved you from going out with women who were boring, crazy, or both. You need to try something new." His face brightening, Doug lifted a finger. "I know. You should try Perfect Match. A client of mine went on one of their adventures, and she swears by the experience."

Marcus winced. Perfect Match evoked images of sleazy matchmakers and desperate women looking for husbands. "That's more commitment than I'm interested in. I'm not looking for a wife."

Doug rolled his eyes. "It's not that kind of a matchmaking site. It's virtual. The AI matches you with a woman it deems perfect for you based on the extensive questionnaires everyone in their database fills out, and you go on a virtual date that feels so real you can't tell it's virtual. You never have to meet the other person in the flesh, and it's so much more than just a date. The session only lasts three hours, but you get to have an adventure that feels like it lasts days or weeks, and you can choose whatever type of experience you want. My client spent a virtual week with a hunky alien on a spaceship."

"With my luck, I will be stuck with some head-case in a virtual world for days on end."

Despite his rebuttal, Marcus was intrigued.

An entirely virtual adventure?

How did that even work?

His expertise was in finance, not computers or artificial intelligence. He only cared about specialized programming insofar as it could give him an edge in the markets.

"You won't get stuck with a head-case," Doug said. "They vet the applicants to ensure that whoever you are matched up with is a good fit and that you are both interested in the same sort of experience. I would have loved to try it, but it's expensive as hell, and I'm saving every penny to open my gym. It's probably chump change for you, though." Doug shrugged. "The question is what you're willing to pay for an experience of a lifetime, huh?"

"Huh," was Marcus's sardonic reply. "I'll think about it."

He'd said it dismissively, but he was still thinking about trying Perfect Match when he showed Doug out, got ready for his day, and was on the way to the office.

Thankfully, hyper-focusing on the job was never a problem for him, and as long as his mind was occupied with stock options, shorts and longs, interest rates, and indexes, Marcus managed to push away thoughts of virtual adventures and perfect dates.

As soon as he had left the office, though, his mind returned to the Perfect Match, and by the time he got home he was committed to researching the subject.

It wouldn't be a waste of time, even if he decided it wasn't for him. The idea was intriguing, and if the experience was as good as Doug had touted it to be, the technology had significant market potential. It might be a worthwhile, untapped investment opportunity.

Was the company traded on an exchange?

Snatching his laptop off his desk, Marcus took it to the living room, sat back on his Corinthian leather couch, loosened his tie, and pulled up the website on the flatscreen in front of him.

"Perfect Match Virtual Fantasy Studios guarantees an unforgettable experience," the sultry female voice purred as the advertisement rolled across the screen. "Set your mind free while your body rests in the perfect safety and comfort of our luxurious studio."

As a tour of their main branch in New York ensued, he realized that it was a mere forty-minute walk from his office, and if he took a taxi, he could be there in less than ten.

They had another location in Los Angeles and plans for opening twenty more next year. That was a rapid expansion, which meant that the company had attracted investment money and a lot of it.

He was definitely going to take a look at their financials.

"Your perfect date with your Perfect Match partner awaits," the sexy actress drawled. "Experience your wildest fantasies without ever having to face your partner in the real world. Your complete anonymity is guaranteed." The woman smiled and leaned closer to the screen as if she was about to reveal a secret. "Thanks to the use of avatars in the virtual adventure, you won't recognize each other even if you meet by chance. Unless you both agree to an in-person meeting, you will never know who the other person was."

That sounded ideal.

"Time moves differently in the virtual world," the spokeswoman continued. "Three hours in the studio could last days or even weeks inside the adventure. It's the perfect vacation solution for busy professionals."

Marcus was busy, but he could spare three hours.

"Let's see what kind of experiences you offer." Marcus clicked out of the introduction video and clicked on the next tab.

There was a Beach Getaway, Ski Vacation, Jungle Cruise…boring.

Those might be good for retirees.

Ah. Here is the good stuff. Star-fighter Battle. Undersea Adventure—as, whoa, merpeople? How did that even work when it came to the physical stuff?

Shaking his head, Marcus kept scrolling.

International Spy—oh, hell yes!

He was a huge James Bond fan. Marcus had seen all the films, read all the books, and even splurged on first editions of Ian Fleming's works signed by the author. Fantasizing about being the debonair Bond and having spy adventures with sexy, dangerous women wasn't something he cared to share with his friends, but he could live the fantasy in the virtual world, and no one would ever be any the wiser.

If the claims of Perfect Match Virtual Studios were to be believed, he could face off against the femme fatale of his creation in a high-stakes adventure, and if the tightening in his pants was anything to go by, his subconscious was thrilled by the idea.

10

MARCUS

The process of getting the Perfect Match adventure scheduled was more involved than Marcus had expected.

The intake forms, the medical review, the credit check—those he'd been ready for, but the questionnaire was a real monster. He'd spent hours answering the hundreds of questions, learning more about himself in the process than he cared to know. Since confidentiality and anonymity were such big selling points for the service, Marcus had been comfortable answering the questions as truthfully as he could.

Some of his answers had surprised him.

Then there was the waiting.

Two weeks had passed since he'd submitted every piece of information possible save for his shoe size, and when he'd finally gotten a call, it wasn't to inform him that his adventure was ready but to tell him that they were still looking for his perfect match.

"You have to be patient, Mr. Shurman," his coordinator said with her well-practiced polite tone. "Your particular set of parameters isn't easily matched, but I assure you that we will find a great partner for you to share the experience with. It will just take a little more time."

"Really?" Marcus hadn't meant to blurt out such an inane question, but he'd been genuinely put out. "Is it because of my chosen adventure?"

Perhaps there weren't many women who dreamt of being Bond girls. The old James Bond movies were a little chauvinistic, but surely the programmers could put a more contemporary spin on the spy adventure and make it exciting for the ladies?

"Not at all, Mr. Shurman," Lesley, his personal coordinator, assured him. "The adventure we are designing for you has broad appeal. We just want to make sure that your partner is the best fit not only for the action sequence of the shared experience but also for the more personal aspects."

Aha. "You're looking for…compatibility."

Sexual preferences, his mind supplied. Not that he'd put down anything particularly wild in that category, but it wasn't purely vanilla, either.

"Correct. Don't worry, Mr. Shurman," she said. "We are getting hundreds of new applications daily, and I'm positive the right partner will turn up soon."

"Let's hope so. Thank you." Marcus ended the call.

It was better to wait for the right partner than to settle for less. Marcus had done that too often in the real world, and he was okay with the Perfect Match people being extra picky about who he shared his virtual adventure with.

He could handle a few more days of waiting. He'd just bury himself in work and try to stop thinking about his perfect mystery lady until they found her.

Right. Easier said than done.

By nightfall, Marcus was a basket case.

Typically, when he was plagued by anxiety, his favorite outlet was women. Going out to a club, zeroing in on a beautiful woman, buying her an expensive drink, dancing with her until they both were so hot and bothered that they couldn't wait to get in bed—

That was how he liked to relax.

Now the thought of going out and finding some nameless woman to waste time on until his fantasy lady was found didn't appeal to him. Who wanted to settle for the mundane when the extraordinary was just around the corner?

It was his damn type-A personality that always pushed him to reach for the best. The problem was that when it came to women, he'd often mistaken the best for the best-looking.

Yeah, he was shallow. Beauty wasn't everything, but since the most beautiful women were also the most coveted by men, he felt like a winner whenever he got a beauty to go home with him.

Maybe Perfect Match was the answer, and the artificial intelligence would do a better job of choosing the right woman for him, one who matched him in intellect and spirit and not just on the scale of attractiveness.

With a sigh, Marcus headed to his home gym instead.

Working off the anxious energy that way would make

his morning routine with Doug hell, but it was better than feeling like shit for compromising on another hookup.

The following two weeks were torture, and when the call he'd been waiting for finally came, a full month after he'd started the intake process, Marcus was in the best shape of his life.

"Did you find a match for me?" He clutched the phone to his ear.

"Yes, Mr. Shurman. I'm delighted to inform you that we've found an excellent match for you to share your virtual adventure with, and we are ready to schedule it. Are you free on—"

"Yes." He would make time for this even if his office went up in smoke. He was done waiting. "Sorry to interrupt. Please, go on."

After the details were hashed out, his coordinator congratulated him again, and then the call ended. The experience was scheduled for Friday evening.

Three hours in the Perfect Match Studio could last as long as three weeks in the virtual world. Could he survive so long playing a superspy?

After the month of boot-camp-style training, hell, yeah!

Marcus was buzzing with excitement, and he wasn't sure which part he was more hyped up for—his Bond adventure or his Perfect Match lady.

Ironically, he didn't care if she was really perfect as long as her avatar in the virtual fantasy precisely matched his desires.

Who needed real-life drama?

It didn't get any better than that.

He had no plans of ever meeting her face to face. But if the adventure turned out as good as the Perfect Match people claimed, he would schedule another one with the same lady if she was so inclined. Hell, he would even pay for her session if finances were a problem.

What made him a little apprehensive, though, was that they would not only look different but would also be different on the inside, with memories and skills that didn't belong to them in the real world. They wouldn't even remember who they were before entering the virtual world and would have a lifetime of experiences downloaded into their brains.

What would she look like in his mind?

What would she be able to do?

Hey, what would he be capable of?

Could he really become a superspy, a James Bond-like figure, someone who saved the day, got the girl, and had a hell of an adventure while doing it?

It was hard to believe that the Perfect Match technology could get every nuance right. But then, not everything was preprogrammed. It wasn't a passive amusement park ride.

His mind and the mind of his partner would drive the adventure, leading it in directions the programmers had never foreseen.

11

MARCUS

Wednesday and Thursday had passed in a blur of introspection and hypothesizing to the point where even the partners at his firm had noticed Marcus's distraction. Thankfully, the boss hadn't been watching him too closely, or she would have reprimanded him.

Or maybe not.

He was good enough at what he was doing to coast on autopilot for a few days and still make a decent profit.

"Hey, Marky-Mark!" Erwin stuck his balding head into his office.

The garish cartoon tie the slimy money manager was wearing hung limply from his scrawny neck. "It's Friday, and me and the boys are heading out to Club G tonight," he went on, completely oblivious of, or perhaps deliberately ignoring, Marcus's frown at the interruption. "You wanna come with? It's been a while since you hung out with us, bro."

Marcus bit back a sigh. Why did so many of his coworkers think it was fun to talk like frat boys? Erwin was thirty-five years old, for God's sake. Furthermore, the guy was married. How did he get away with partying after work with the bachelors?

Perhaps his wife didn't give a damn about what he was doing.

Hell, she might be happy to get him out of her hair. It wasn't as if the guy was pleasant to be around.

"Thanks, but I've got other plans for tonight."

"Oh yeah?" Erwin's slimy grin got wider. "You got a lady on the hook? Reeling in some sweet little pu—"

"Mr. Gallagher!"

"Aw shit," Erwin muttered before turning to look at Mrs. Cage's scowling face.

Diminutive and in her sixties, Marjorie Cage didn't look like the powerhouse woman who owned one of Wall Street's most successful money management firms. But everyone working in her office was well aware of who their boss was and what her expectations of them were. If they failed to meet them, she had no qualms about showing her displeasure by shoving them out the door.

Mrs. Cage had very firm ideas about what topics of conversation were appropriate for the workplace, and everyone who valued their place in her firm made sure to watch their language around her.

"Mr. Gallagher," she said coldly, "unless you're talking about a cat, I don't want to hear that sort of language in my office. Are we clear?"

"Yes, ma'am," he replied, keeping his eyes low.

"Is it your lunch break?"

"No, ma'am."

"Are you on any sort of legally mandated break?"

"No, ma'am."

She looked him up and down with a frown. "Then I believe you should be at your desk, working, right?"

As the guy scurried off, Mrs. Cage turned to Marcus. "You shouldn't indulge his nonsense. You're one of the best managers at this firm, and he's wasting your time."

Erwin Gallagher was a distant relation of hers, which was why he was still employed.

"Yes, ma'am," Marcus agreed quickly.

With one last piercing look, Mrs. Cage stalked back down the hallway.

The woman was the queen of the backhanded compliment. Or maybe it had been a threat. Either way, Marcus was happy that she'd dismissed Erwin for him.

The guy was the husband of her niece or something like that, so as long as he put in some minimal effort he could prance around the office with no fear of getting fired, and since no one wanted to step on Marjorie's toes, Erwin felt like he had a license to keep digging for gossip and not taking a damn hint.

Glancing at his watch, Marcus let out a sigh.

Four more hours to go.

He just needed to make it to the end of the day. Then he'd get out of there, head straight to the Perfect Match Studio, settle into the experience of a lifetime, and forget all about bad dates and office politics for a few hours.

12

MARCUS

By the time Marcus made it to the Perfect Match Studio, he was running fifteen minutes late despite the taxi driver's best attempts to weave through the congested traffic.

He should have left work early and walked there.

James Bond wouldn't have to deal with rush-hour traffic. He would have swerved around the other cars while somehow miraculously avoiding pedestrians or hopped onto a random motorcycle and cruised down the center line without a single ding.

"Mr. Shurman." The woman behind the desk smiled and rose to her feet.

He recognized his personal coordinator's voice. Lesley was dressed surprisingly casually, but it did nothing to diminish the force of her bubbly personality.

She offered him her hand. "Welcome to the Perfect Match Studios. It's a pleasure to finally meet you in person."

Her friendly but professional greeting was a disappointment. Usually, women gave him a thorough look over and then started to flirt.

Maybe Lesley was married?

He glanced at her hand, looking for a wedding ring, but she had so many on that it was hard to tell if any of them was what he was looking for.

Besides, he should be thankful for her professional attitude. The woman must have read his answered questionnaire, which meant that she knew more about him than his own mother, but if she had any criticism, it didn't show on her face. She was either very well trained or entirely nonjudgmental.

"Same here." Marcus shook her hand. "Is my match already here?"

His partner could be in their other location in Los Angeles, but he had a gut feeling that she was a New Yorker like him.

"We're still waiting for her to arrive." Lesley motioned for him to follow her. "But we can get you prepped and have your adventure underway before we bring her into the experience." She led him down a hallway with high-end blue carpeting and eggshell-white painted walls.

Marcus frowned. "Are you sure that she's on her way?"

She wasn't thinking of canceling, was she?

It had taken a month to get his first match, and he didn't want to wait for another one to finally have the experience he was paying so much for. Plus, even though he knew he'd be meeting only her avatar in the virtual adventure, not the woman herself, he couldn't help being intensely curious about her.

What sort of person would she be? A finance pro like him, a student with a hefty trust fund, a doctor, a lawyer?

"I'm sure," the coordinator said as they entered a sterile-looking room.

The chair that occupied most of the space reminded him of the dentist's office, and the wall behind it was lined with a raft of equipment. A technician was seated on a stool beside the chair, wearing pristine, pale blue scrubs.

"Good afternoon." The guy greeted Marcus with a broad smile. "I'm David, and I will be monitoring you throughout the experience."

"Thank you." Marcus offered David his hand.

Lesley walked over to the chair and put her hand on the strange-looking helmet. "Even with your partner's slight delay, we will make sure to give you the complete experience you paid for, Mr. Shurman. Naturally, we won't charge extra for the time you spend in the virtual world by yourself, and it will lend even more verisimilitude to your interaction with your partner." She gestured to the chair again. "Are you ready to begin?"

"Very much so." What else could he say?

Even though Marcus was somewhat apprehensive, he would never allow himself to show weakness.

As she gave him a look over, the twisting of her lips told him that it wasn't for the reason he usually got those. "Haven't you read our instruction email about wearing comfortable clothing? I can give you a pair of scrubs if you'd like."

He had read the email, but he wasn't going to show up in sweats.

"Thank you for the offer, but I'm fine. Everything I'm wearing was custom-tailored for me. It's very comfortable."

"Of course." Lesley put on her practiced smile.

Marcus let her take his jacket and tie, slipped his shoes off, and after a moment, decided to take his belt off as well. By the time he was sitting back in the chair, he felt almost naked. He'd stripped off his expensive, professional armor piece by piece until he was left in his trousers, socks, and a dress shirt. The Tom Ford was unbuttoned to his navel, so the tech could stick the countless wires to his chest, and one sleeve rolled up so the technician could access his veins.

"Let's go over a few basics," David said. "What's your avatar's name?"

"William Kentworth."

"How old are you?"

"Thirty-four." That was his actual age, and he'd chosen to stick with it.

"What's your safe word?"

"Bulldog."

The tech cracked a smile. "No one has ever used that one before. Hold it in your mind for a moment and visualize the dog. You will have a difficult time remembering it inside your adventure, but you won't need it. If your vitals show any distress, I'll stop the program long before you even think to use your safe word."

Marcus arched a brow. "I asked for a James Bond-style adventure. I'm sure my vitals will be all over the place when I run away from explosions and evade assassins." Not to mention the other stuff he'd be doing.

"Don't worry. I'm not going to stop the program unless

you reach a level your body can't handle. Never happened to me before, and I've been doing this since the studios first opened. The adventures are designed with participants' health in mind."

"That's reassuring." Marcus shivered as the tech cleaned the inside of his elbow with an alcohol wipe.

"Would you like a heated blanket?" David asked.

"No." On the other hand... "Actually, yes."

"You've got it, sir." He carefully inserted the IV needle. "You've got great veins," he added as he taped the IV in place. "Don't fight going under. Let the experience come to you."

"Okay," Marcus said dryly.

As he watched the man move away, he was already starting to feel a little drowsy. By the time the warm, heavy blanket settled over his body, he could barely keep his eyes open. Remembering the tech's advice, Marcus took a deep breath and relaxed.

13

MARIAN

I can't do this.

Marian hadn't meant to back down. She really hadn't. She'd come to the Perfect Match studio intending to go through with the experience, to go on the adventure of her dreams and meet her perfect match. But as she'd settled into the chair and the technician swiped her arm with an alcohol wipe in preparation for the IV, her anxiety spiked, and she balked.

What if something went wrong?

What if they fried her brain?

What if she couldn't wake up?

What if she didn't remember who she was when she got out of the virtual world?

"Stop."

The technician frowned. "Is something wrong?"

Yes. What the hell am I doing?

Am I so pathetic that I need to have fun virtually because I can't have it in reality?

"I'm not sure this is for me."

"Oh." The technician's eyes went wide. "Oh, um... I'm sorry, I'm really not equipped to handle...that is, I can get your experience coordinator for you if you'd like, and—"

"Yes, please." Marian knew she was going to have to pay a hefty penalty for backing out at the last minute, but it was a price she was willing to pay if it meant saving her brain and maintaining her dignity.

The studios had a perfect safety record, and no one's brains had been fried so far, so that was not a logical fear.

It was her damn pride.

As she watched the frazzled technician scuttle out the door, she wondered what the panic attack was about.

Was it really about dignity? Or was it about fear? About confronting and accepting her own needs?

Marian was terrible at making real human connections, and it was time she acknowledged that it was a weakness. Her need to always be in control was one of the main reasons she had trouble making friends and maintaining romantic relationships, and it was also the reason she was terrified of letting a machine take over her mind.

It's safe. It's perfectly safe.

This is my chance to have the most exciting experience of my life, and I'm balking for no good reason other than the fear of the unknown.

She had to do it or forever regret chickening out.

What was that damn buzzing sound?

It took a moment for her to realize that it was her phone ringing. As instructed, she'd silenced it, but she could still hear the buzzing from where she'd left her purse.

With a sigh, she reached for it.

She wasn't supposed to take calls in here, but what the hell. She'd already decided to back out of this. "This is Marian Ferber," she answered the call.

"Marian!"

It was Gigi, and she sounded off. Sad. Probably drunk. Marian sighed. It wasn't the first time one of her clients had called her in a state, and she never enjoyed it.

"Gigi," she said politely. "Aren't you with the boys tonight?"

"No! That cheating bar…bat…buster…anyway, that guy, he's got them tonight! He actually asked for time with them, an' I couldn't say no, not when the boys were so excited for that rat…buster…to spend some time with 'em…"

"Ah. Then perhaps you should—"

"So, I went out instead! Time for me to be on the town, live large, live it up! But, Marian." Gigi began to sob. "I jus', I hate bars. I hate clubs. I wanna be at home with my boys, with all my boys, an' now I can't. I hate it, I hate it, how could he do this to me?"

"Gigi, hon, you need to call your sister, all right? Have her come get you."

"You come get me," Gigi insisted.

Marian pictured it, leaving this place and driving to a crowded bar to pick up her drunk, clingy client, probably spending hours getting her settled and listening to her woes yet again. It was the antithesis of fun.

This is what the real world has to offer you right now.

"Miss Ferber?" Her coordinator walked through the door, looking a little pissed off. "I'm sorry, but we can't allow you to make calls from here. If you've decided not to participate in the experience, you need to hang up and come back to the lobby with me."

Marian stared at her for a long moment.

She thought about what was waiting for her outside those doors.

Then she thought of what might be waiting for her right now, the person who was ready to share a great experience with her. If she walked out, she'd be letting down not only herself but the guy she'd been matched with as well.

"I'm so sorry," she said. "Let me finish this, and then we can get started. I panicked momentarily, but I'm fine now and ready to proceed."

The woman nodded.

"Gigi," Marian said to her client, "I've got to go. Call your sister. It'll be okay, I promise."

"But—"

Marian ended the call before the woman could try to persuade her otherwise, then shot off a text to Gigi's sister and her mother before turning her phone completely off. "I'm ready," she said, lying back in the chair. "Let's do this."

"Excellent! I'll get our tech back."

It took slightly longer than a moment, and the tech took a few minutes to review her avatar's name and other pertinent details.

"Claudette Roth," the tech confirmed. "Age twenty-eight. The sole heiress to the Roth family fortune."

"That's me." Marian smiled. "The most notorious and glamorous jewel thief."

14

CLAUDETTE

Present time in the virtual adventure...

Can this night get any worse?
Claudette couldn't believe that she'd gotten caught by some arrogant bastard in a bad suit.

Truth be told, the suit wasn't half bad, and from what she'd glimpsed, the body it covered was spectacular. Not that she'd taken the time to stop and admire her captor's physique as he'd chased after her, or when she'd pummeled him.

"After you, darling." He manhandled her into the back of a black car that had arrived shortly after the helicopter had taken off and then slid right in next to her.

All right, maybe she'd taken a little time to admire him. After all, she would need to be dead not to notice the bloody man's rugged good looks.

Did he have to smell so divine? Since when could government agents afford such expensive cologne?

It wasn't a scent Claudette recognized, and given that she hobnobbed with lords and billionaires, she was familiar with all the luxury brands. It also wasn't often that she was impressed enough by a man to pay him attention beyond what she could get from him. But this one, Agent Kentworth, if she recalled correctly, had quite a lot going for him.

His dark brown hair was thick and well-groomed, contrasting beautifully with the brilliant blue of his eyes, and when he smiled with that broad mouth and those high cheekbones of his, he looked like sin itself.

She'd hit one of those lovely cheekbones quite hard.

Glancing at the bruise, Claudette winced and looked at her handcuffed hands. Her knuckles were bruised and hurt like hell, probably more than his face, which had felt as if it had been carved from stone.

She didn't regret it, though. He deserved it and then some. Someone needed to bring that infuriating arrogance of his down a notch. Nevertheless, she did hate to mar such a pretty canvas.

As his lips twitched with a smile, she huffed out a breath, shifted in her seat, and spent the rest of the ride looking out the window. She wouldn't give the wanker the satisfaction of openly admiring him.

When they reached headquarters, he escorted her to an ugly room, which was done up all in beige, and left her there without removing the handcuffs and without saying a word.

Was that his idea of torture?

The floor, walls, and ceiling colors matched with such precision that she knew it was intentional. It was a room designed to lull her into a stupor, to have her lower her guard and slip into a state of mild discomfort.

It was intended to bore.

Bored people talked more, desperate to fill the void it inspired.

Well, the joke was on them. Claudette had lived through years' worth of afternoon teas with the most droning, painfully nasal, utterly dreary buffoons that England had to offer. Silence was golden by comparison, and at least there were no cake stands here.

As the beige door opened, Claudette's heart raced for a split second before she realized it wasn't her handsome captor. This was a shorter man, older, with a very shiny bald head and a pair of gold-rimmed spectacles that were so reflective they made it hard to see his eyes.

"Good evening, Miss Roth," he said politely as he sat down across from her.

"Or is it morning?" she asked idly.

"Not quite." He glanced at his watch, a cheap digital affair. "It's two-thirty-seven a.m. Not what I'd call proper morning."

"Hmm."

"Are you very tired?" he asked, setting a file down on the table between them. "Would you care for some tea?"

She smiled. "I would love some tea. Darjeeling, please, steeped for three minutes only, with half a teaspoon of sugar and no milk."

He nodded but made no move to get up, so she assumed that either her request wasn't going to be carried out or someone was listening in.

Of course they were. The mirror on the wall wasn't actually a mirror. Someone was watching her, and she wouldn't be surprised if it was William Kentworth. He'd pretended not to be aware of her during the ride, but she knew it had been an act.

Agent Kentworth was very much interested in her, and not just for her thieving skills.

Claudette folded her cuffed hands in her lap and waited for the man to speak.

"Miss Roth, my name is Liam Grable. I'm with the Secret Intelligence Service. And you," he paused and smiled, "you're something of a problem for us."

"I assure you I don't intend to be," she said as politely as she could manage. "Tonight was just a massive misunderstanding. I'm sure my solicitor can help make that clear if you would just let me contact him. I do believe that's my right."

"It would be if we didn't have indisputable physical evidence tying you to breaking into Clarence House tonight. DNA evidence, to be precise."

Damn.

She'd worn gloves, and her hair had been covered, but she'd pulled her full-face mask off when she'd entered the bedroom and run a hand through her ponytail. She could have shed a few hairs. And then she'd scratched an itch on her nose and might have dislodged a few skin cells. Did they go through the room with a microscope?

Not likely. Grable was bluffing.

"You haven't had time to find DNA evidence, let alone analyze it."

He smiled again, his glasses gleaming. He had very white teeth. "We've got excellent equipment, Miss Roth. I assure you, our results are conclusive and will stand up in a court of law."

"You could have planted the evidence."

"We could have, but we didn't." He opened up the folder between them and began spreading out some regrettably familiar photos. "And with this DNA evidence confirming your identity, we can tie you to a series of high-profile burglaries that have occurred across not only the United Kingdom but most of Europe. Diamonds in Brussels, sapphires in Germany, a very impressive cache of lapis lazuli artifacts in Hungary—" He lifted his gaze to her. "You've been a very busy woman, Miss Roth."

A chill began sweeping through Claudette's body, starting at her face.

Getting caught had always been a possibility, and it was part of the thrill, challenging her to come up with fail-proof stunts, but after years of successful heists, she'd started to feel invincible and had gotten sloppy.

She should have quit while she'd been ahead, she'd even tried, but like a bloody addict, she'd become so restless that she felt like crawling out of her own skin. Nothing else could scratch that itch, and she'd kept taking on ever more dangerous jobs.

Claudette forced her numb lips to move. "I demand to

see my solicitor at once. You have no right to keep me here without him being present."

Grable shook his head. "You've proved that you're a danger to king and country with your performance tonight, Miss Roth. With the evidence we've compiled, you could be going away for a very long time. Decades at least. More, if the prosecutors want to charge you with espionage or attempted murder."

"I didn't attempt to murder anyone!" Claudette snapped. "And I'm not a spy!"

"Miss Roth." Grable's voice was ice cold. "You made your way into the heart of one of the royal family's personal residences. The potential for damage to person, not to mention property, is incalculable. It doesn't matter that you didn't plant a bomb or lace the pillowcases with poison."

Claudette began to shake internally, and she prayed it wasn't showing externally. The noose was tightening around her neck, and she didn't see a way out. Not this time. They had built an iron-clad case against her, and if she didn't do what they wanted her to do, she was going to spend the rest of her life in prison.

Grable leaned over the table. "The point is that you could have planted a bomb in the building or done any sort of damage. Do you understand what I'm saying?"

Loud and clear. What he was actually saying was, *if we say jump, you can only ask how high.*

Claudette cleared her throat. "I have no interest in causing anyone harm," she said as firmly as she could. "I swear."

"I believe you," Grable replied, all mild-mannered again.

"Over fifteen jobs, and not a single person injured until now."

She frowned. "You're not talking about your agent, are you? Because he threatened to shoot me, and—"

"And by the time you got around to hitting him, you knew he didn't have a gun."

"He could have been lying."

"Will is very good at that," Grable allowed. "But he wasn't."

Claudette sighed. She was tired, she was stressed, and she wanted her bloody tea. "What exactly do you want from me, hmm? You've got me over a barrel, and I know it, so you might as well just tell me and save us some time."

"What we want, Miss Roth, is your expertise." Grable smiled. It was a polite smile, but she knew that it concealed daggers. "Your persona, if you will. It's an open secret in intelligence circles that you're a jewel thief of some renown. We want to leverage that reputation to take down one of the most dangerous weapons dealers in the world."

Oh Lord. "You've lost me completely."

"Allow me to elaborate."

15

WILLIAM

His cheek throbbing and his eye feeling bigger than his entire head, William sat in the room adjacent to the interrogation room and watched Claudette Roth through the two-way mirror.

He should have gone home and gotten some sleep, but he couldn't bring himself to leave her in Liam's hands.

Not that there was anything wrong with his handler. The guy was professional and leve-lheaded, and he would treat the thief like a lady regardless of her chosen occupation.

She was perfectly safe with him.

Mark walked into the room and handed William an ice pack. "Put it on."

"Thank you." He took the pack without taking his eyes off the woman on the other side of the mirror. "Are you here because of her?" he asked the agent.

"Regrettably, I'm not assigned to her case. I was just curious," Mark admitted. "I've heard a lot about the notorious jewel thief and the efforts to trap her. Finally, we have her just where we want her."

Given Claudette's pinched expression, she was starting to realize the pickle she was in, and her confident veneer was starting to crack.

William should feel satisfaction, but all he felt was a dim sense of regret.

The woman had gotten him good, more than once, and he was wearing the evidence on his face and on his bruised abs. But instead of wanting to see her pay, he regretted seeing her squirm. He also regretted not removing her cuffs.

She wasn't a dangerous criminal, and she wouldn't have attacked Liam. Leaving the cuffs on had been petty revenge, and he felt guilty for doing so.

"Pretty girl, ain't she?" Mark leaned back in his chair. "What makes a rich sweet thing like her engage in such a dangerous activity?"

"Beats me," William murmured. "She's a vicious little creature. I never expected her to have such a mean hook."

Mark chuckled. "You were being a gentleman. You could have knocked her out with one punch or tackled her to the ground and had her in handcuffs, ready to ship out. Instead, you let her punch you." The agent slanted an amused glance at him. "Would you have been so reserved if she were ugly?"

"Of course. I don't hit ladies." William winced. "Even when they don't act very ladylike."

"Right." Mark crossed his arms over his chest. "What about female agents? We've both gotten in some punches."

"That was different. They had protective gear on, and it was done for training. Our enemies won't hold back because they are females, and they need to practice sparring with males."

"Well, from now on, you need to think of Claudette Roth as a fellow agent. The assignment Liam is sending her on will require intensive training."

"Not by me." William moved the ice pack to his swollen eye. "She will be someone else's problem."

He was a senior operative, and training rookies wasn't his job. So why was he getting angry at the thought of someone else preparing Claudette for the dangerous mission she was about to undertake?

The woman was beautiful and overconfident in her abilities. She would walk all over a less experienced agent, which would be detrimental to her success and might get her killed.

"Who does Liam have in mind for her?" he asked.

"Not me." Mark uncrossed his arms and leaned forward. "Which is a shame because I would love to get a piece of that."

The guy was happily married, so it was just macho boasting, but it aggravated William nonetheless.

"Don't!" he said with a vehemence that surprised him. "That's no way to talk about a lady."

Mark frowned. "Says the guy who just a week ago said—"

William lifted his hand. "Don't repeat that. It was crass, and I regret those words ever leaving my mouth."

"The woman must have hit you harder than I thought." Mark leaned to examine the bruise on William's cheek. "Perhaps you should get checked for concussion."

William pushed Mark's face away. "I'm getting older. That kind of language no longer suits me. And since you are my age, you shouldn't talk like that either."

Laughing, Mark slapped his knee. "If I dared to talk like that at home, my wife would do much worse to me than what Claudette Roth has done to you. But you are a bachelor, William. Enjoy it while you can." He cast another look at the two-way mirror. "You have to admit, though. She's a looker."

"Yeah, she is. It's a shame she's a thief. I don't get involved with criminals."

Mark's lips twitched with a smile. "I didn't say anything about involvement."

16

CLAUDETTE

The more Liam Grable talked, the worse Claudette's sense of impending doom became.

The man they intended her to steal from was a Russian national named Grigoriy Volkov. He was a former member of the KGB who, upon retirement, had turned his acquired knowledge into a lucrative international arms trade.

Even though Volkov mostly stole the goods he traded from the Russian military, his close personal relationship with the Russian president made him untouchable. No one dared to investigate him, not even in this case when the goods had the word nuclear in their name.

"Wait, no, stop right there." Claudette shook her head. "Are you having a laugh? Absolutely not. I want nothing to do with someone who deals in nukes."

"Volkov does not deal in nuclear bombs, Ms. Roth," Grable said, like that made a difference. "Only the triggers."

"They are still part of a nuclear bomb!"

Grable let out a long-suffering sigh. "It is not the same.

The triggers can't explode on their own, and they don't contain any nuclear material. You won't be exposed to any radiation or be near any explosives."

She hated to ask, but... "What do you want me to do? Find out who the buyer is? Or maybe steal the schematics for how to build the triggers?"

Liam leaned back and offered her the first genuine smile so far. "That would not be suitable for your particular set of skills, Ms. Roth. We want you to steal Mr. Volkov's priceless collection of imperial Fabergé eggs. He has the world's largest private collection, second only to the Kremlin Armory Museum."

Claudette's interest was piqued. Fabergé eggs. That was right up her alley. Except, why was MI6 interested in them?

Was the economy so bad that the secret service was gearing up for alternative ways to fund its operations?

If she could, she would cross her arms over her chest, but her wrists were still cuffed. "Am I being used as a distraction while someone else is going for the important stuff?"

"You are as clever as your dossier claims, Ms. Roth. Stealing the eggs is only a cover for what you will actually be doing, which is uploading spyware onto Volkov's computer and planting a listening device in his home office. However, when you're caught—"

"What?" She was lost again. "Why would I get caught? I don't get caught." Grable opened his mouth, but she cut him off. "Tonight was a combination of bad luck and getting ratted out by that maid, and don't try to deny that she helped you."

"I won't. It was the maid," he acknowledged.

"So then, why don't I just plant the bug and the software and get out?"

"Mr. Volkov is a paranoid man, and his mansion is near-impenetrable. Given the high likelihood of capture, we need an operative who has another viable objective. With your love of stealing gems and jewels, you have the perfect one. When you're caught with your hand in the safe, Volkov won't suspect that you were after anything other than his precious eggs."

Claudette's blood ran cold. "So you do intend for me to be caught."

"We want to anticipate the worst. And naturally, there are plans in place to account for that possibility." Grable softened his tone and assumed a fatherly expression she didn't appreciate. "You wouldn't be doing this alone. We would assign our best agent to accompany you and see to it that you're not only recovered but that you get back home safely. At which point, we will expunge your record and set you free with nary a second glance."

Relief washed over her. There was a way out, provided that the Russian didn't kill her and that she turned in her burglary tools and assumed the role society expected of her.

That was just another kind of death. Her soul would shrivel and die.

Grable scowled and tapped his earpiece. "Yes. You heard right... it's you. Yes. No."

"Are you talking to me?" she asked.

He shook his head. "I'm sorry. Where were we?"

"You said you would set me free after this mission and clear my record."

"That's right," Grable confirmed.

"As long as I stop stealing, I suppose," Claudette said sourly.

"At the very least you will have to stop stealing from British nationals, yes."

So she could steal abroad. That was good, but it still sounded like a suicide mission. Claudette was well acquainted with the oligarch class in Russian circles, and they were mercurially violent, perpetually hungry sharks who were constantly snapping at each other's heels, ready to bite one another in half at the first sign of weakness. She loathed them passionately and had no problem admitting that she also fiercely feared them.

She would be daft not to.

There would be no mercy just because she was an attractive woman. On the other hand, she didn't want to be sent to prison to rot the rest of her youth away either. There was too much Claudette had yet to accomplish, and given how things were with her father right now, she couldn't allow herself to be locked up.

Responsibility was looming, closer than ever, unstoppable like a meteor falling to earth. The only question was, how bad would the fallout be?

"Who is your best agent anyhow?" she asked, pretending to inspect her nails. Ugh, she'd chipped two of them during her flight. "How can I believe that this person could protect me against a man you paint as being paranoid to the point of probably having his own private army? It sounds undoable."

"Ah, well." Grable brightened a bit. "You've already met him, actually. It's Agent Kentworth." As Claudette groaned, the door opened, and in walked that bloody tall pillock of a man. Of course, it had to be him! This night was going from bad to worse. Or was it this day already?

How long had she been in that beige torture chamber with the blindingly shiny bald head?

Kentworth had a cup of tea in one hand and a shit-eating grin on his face. "Oh, I'm sorry. I didn't mean to interrupt," he said with perfect insincerity as he walked over to the table and set the tea in front of her. "I just wanted to bring you this."

Against her better judgment, Claudette inspected the tea. The scent proclaimed it to be Darjeeling, and the color made it appear as though it had been steeped for precisely three minutes. When Agent Kentworth kindly unlocked the cuffs binding her wrists she picked up the cup and took a sip.

Lightly sweet and perfectly hot, just how she liked it.

How had this man timed his arrival so perfectly?

Whatever, it didn't matter. What mattered was that Claudette wanted nothing to do with this bloke. "Who else have you got?" She kept her gaze on Grable, ignoring Agent Kentworth as best she could, at which she was failing miserably. He was like a magnet to her eyes. "If he's the best you've got, you've got much larger problems than the oligarch."

Grable laughed as his agent scowled.

"I was good enough to catch you," Kentworth pointed out.

"Barely."

"Caught is caught. Don't split hairs just because you don't like the outcome."

"I don't like the prospect of working with you, that's what I don't like."

It had nothing to do with the fact that he'd caught her when no one else had ever come close, or that despite the growing shiner on his face, he was one of the most stunningly attractive men she'd ever seen.

He was annoyingly perfect. If she could draw her dream guy, he would look like Agent Kentworth, except, the man of her dreams had turned out to be the man of her nightmares.

"I'm afraid neither of you has a choice," Grable put in before Agent Kentworth could respond. "It will take a very particular skill set to pull this mission off successfully. William is uniquely qualified for it."

"Oh, is he? Because, what, he speaks Russian and can crawl through underbrush toting a rifle with the best of them?" Claudette drawled. "That can hardly be an exclusive club in the SIS."

"Not at all," Grable agreed blandly. "But what William can do in addition to that that no one else can handle, is pre-mission training for a completely green operative like yourself."

Claudette nearly choked on her tea. "What? No!"

Agent Kentworth turned an incredulous eye on Grable. "You want me to train her too? You can't be serious."

"I'm quite serious," Grable told both of them. "This operation is of the utmost secrecy. While many throughout the agency know that we've apprehended Miss Roth, almost none of them know what we plan to do with her. This requirement for secrecy comes from the highest level of our agency and is non-negotiable. The fewer people who know what Miss Roth is training for, the better."

He stared at her, unblinking, his eyes perfectly visible for once behind those glaring lenses. "Miss Roth, let me be blunt. If you choose not to cooperate with us, you will be imprisoned for at least the next twenty years. But if you do, you will not only be a free woman in as little as a month, you will contribute substantially to the greater safety and well-being of the entire globe."

Claudette's mouth snapped shut.

Twenty years...

She couldn't do that. Nothing was worth it. And there was nothing she wouldn't do to avoid that, even suffer through training with the smug-faced, irritatingly handsome agent.

"Why a month? Why not sooner?" She had somewhere very important to be in a month.

Grable smiled. "If you think you can get through Agent Kentworth's training in less than a month, you're welcome to try. I would be most surprised, however."

Judging from said agent's disgruntled expression, he agreed.

Well then. That settled Claudette's motivation. She would do this in under a month, even if it killed her.

"It's a deal."

17

WILLIAM

In a remote mansion situated in the Yorkshire Dales, William watched one of the five monitors in the control center as Claudette worked her way toward the office.

Pressure plate beneath the carpet—check.
Lasers—check.

Excellent, she remembered to spray for them this time. As he watched her avoid them with all the dexterity of an acrobat, William could not keep a little smile off his face. She'd really gotten the hang of those.

Not that it seemed difficult for her.

Claudette was truly gifted. She combined a level of grace and athleticism that one rarely saw so well developed.

After reluctantly taking on the assignment, William had learned a few things about her that he wished he had known before making an unflattering assessment of her character, which had been totally off the mark.

Claudette had trained as an elite gymnast up to the age

of nineteen, had awards in both horsemanship and archery and had achieved a second, less publicized degree in Computer Engineering. She was talented and hard-working, and even without her natural beauty, she had the potential to be a mover in the world.

With it? She could be a force to be reckoned with.

Beepbeepbeepbeep—

"Shit!"

Of course, all the potential in the world didn't mean much when one lacked patience and was inclined to rush things.

William shut off the alarm she'd triggered by opening the office door. "Again. From the top."

"No!" Claudette snapped, turning and staring at him through the nearest camera. "From here. I know how to handle this alarm. I just—"

"This is not a computer game, and you aren't going to get a redo in the field or an additional life. It's all or nothing, and so far today, you've set off the alarm five times. That's a lot of nothing."

"I just forgot! Let me start from here this once, and I'll—"

"Go. Back. To. The. Beginning."

Raising her hand toward the camera in a two-finger salute, she turned and stalked back down the perfectly-replicated corridor of Volkov's home.

William massaged the space between his eyes where a tension headache had been gathering all morning. Two weeks in, and he was finding it harder and harder to deal with his beautiful charge alone.

The beginning of training had been simple enough. He'd

put her through a series of tests to assess her abilities, so he could design her training to get her where she needed to be.

With one exception, she'd performed exceedingly well.

Claudette was a terrible shot with a pistol, which was baffling since she was a dedicated archer. How she could have such a terrible aim was a mystery to him.

Still, that was something that could be overcome easily enough. He'd moved them away from headquarters and to this place, a training facility continually reworked according to whatever mission was currently top priority. The facility housed a cook, a caretaker, and the two of them.

On the face of things, it was the perfect place to buckle down and focus, but in reality, it had turned out to be his own special hell.

With no one to spend time with but each other, he had quickly become...what? Entranced was too strong a word. Intrigued, perhaps. Interested. Somewhat infatuated.

Yeah, right. Turned on like a damn lightbulb. A whole floor's worth of them.

It was solely the product of being in close quarters with a beautiful woman day in and day out, thinking about her at night when he couldn't fall asleep and wondering if she was thinking about him as she lay awake.

It was folly, completely unprofessional, and went against regulations.

For both their sakes, he needed to keep his distance.

It wasn't about professional decorum. Their lives depended on it.

With a sigh, William reset the course and watched Claudette start again from the ballroom.

She evaded the robots, which were a bunch of specially programmed Roombas meant to indicate staff members, picked someone's pocket to get a keycard, got into the private wing of Volkov's mansion, then made her way toward his office.

Pressure plate, lasers...she almost made a mistake there, righting herself barely in time to avoid tripping one of them.

William glanced at his watch and grimaced. They were two hours into this. She needed a break.

Right after this attempt.

Claudette reached the office door, opened it a crack, and pulled out a slender blade. Snipping the hair-thin trigger line attached on the inside, she slipped into the office.

Excellent.

William felt his chest swell with pride.

She found the laptop hidden in the desk drawer, and from there, it was a simple matter of turning it on and uploading the file.

Fantastic.

The next task was placing the listening device, which was a little tricky since MI6 didn't have the layout of Volkov's private office.

They'd extrapolated from intel they had on his other properties and introduced a similar theme into their model.

Claudette looked around, pulling several books off the shelf and then walking over to check some of the decorative pieces. She settled on the bronze statue of a horse and planted the bug at the base of it. When she crept for the door, William turned off the program, which also turned the regular lights on.

He'd expected Claudette to be pleased that she was done for now. Instead, she threw her hands up in the air and turned toward one of the cameras. "Why did you stop the program?" She looked irritated. "I can keep going!"

"You've done very well," William congratulated her. "It's time for a break."

"I don't need a break."

"Your performance on that last round with the lasers says you do." He'd attempted to be light-hearted with it, but from the way she scowled, he'd clearly missed the mark. "Not that it wasn't good. But—"

"Oh, shove it." Claudette jerked the door open and strode down the hall.

Once she got back to the ballroom, she didn't head to the control center where William was or even the kitchen where Mrs. Wainwright was currently making supper. No, she strode straight for the front door that would take her outside and into the currently abysmal weather that had blown in last night.

She didn't even have her wellies on and was trudging through the mud in her high heels.

"Damn it." William rose to his feet and headed out after her.

He, at least, stopped to get his wellies on, as well as a rain jacket and an umbrella.

"Agent Kentworth?" Mrs. Wainwright stopped him on the verge of shutting the door.

He sighed, then turned to look back at her. "Yes?"

"Would you tell Miss Roth I've prepared her favorite for tonight?"

She had? How did Mrs. Wainwright even know Claudette's favorite food?

"Certainly." He started to close the door.

"Hold on." She came over and stuffed something wrapped in a napkin into William's pocket. "Please give this to her. It'll warm her up a treat."

"Thank you."

The elderly woman gave him a smile and a sharp pat on the cheek. "You're quite welcome. Best be gone now before you lose track of her."

Not that Claudette had anywhere to go, but the point was well taken. He headed out into the rain, pausing briefly under the canopy of upland ash trees that the caretaker here had resolutely kept alive despite the threat of disease going through the population.

He began walking west, following the deep indents Claudette's high heels had left in the grass.

18

WILLIAM

*B*y the time William caught up to Claudette, enough time had passed that she was soaked through.

Her arms clasped tight across her chest, she stood at the edge of the little hill that climbed a hundred feet higher than the house it sheltered. Seemingly oblivious to the rain, she stared out into the misty afternoon.

Wet through as she was, it took him a moment to realize that her face was wet not only from raindrops but also from tears.

Why was she crying?

It wasn't his business, and he should keep a professional distance, but she was cold and wet, and he couldn't just leave her there.

Standing next to her, William unfolded the umbrella and held it aloft so that it covered both of them. On second thought, he shrugged off the raincoat and wrapped it around her shoulders.

That seemed to startle her out of whatever trance she'd been in.

She looked at him with wide eyes. "What—oh." Her hands moved to clasp the edge of the coat and draw it in a little tighter. "Now you're going to be the wet one," she sighed.

"Wouldn't be the first time," William said easily.

Surely it didn't count as breaching the distance between them if he inquired about her state of mind? After all, her welfare was one of his top concerns. "What went wrong in there? Why didn't you want to take a break?"

"Because," she said with a sniff. "I didn't need one."

"But you did. You've been doing very draining mental and physical work for over two hours. Giving yourself a moment to refuel and catch your breath is nothing to be ashamed of. In fact, it's necessary." He looked at her a little more closely. "Why are you pushing so hard?"

Claudette sighed. "I thought you'd be happy I was pushing myself."

"It's my job as your trainer to push you at just the right rate to be ready for the job according to the timeline. I've got that aspect of things under control."

"Your timeline sucks."

Ah, he was onto something here. "What's your rush? What is it that you need to be available for?"

"That's none of your business," Claudette said, but her voice was thready. Weak. Exhausted.

She was nearing burnout.

He had been wrong to think that she was progressing so fast effortlessly. It was likely the result of intense focus and determination, but it had come at a cost. He should have paid more attention and noticed she was nearing a breaking point. This was his fault, and he needed to fix it.

"Claudette. Please." The urge to reach for her was nearly overwhelming. "Talk to me. Tell me how I can help you."

"Let me work," she pleaded.

Hearing the desperation in her voice slew him.

"Let me do what you're asking of me!" She turned a pair of pleading eyes on him. "I'm sure I can learn all this in less than a month. I have to."

"Tell me why?"

When she kept her lips resolutely sealed, William gave in to the impulse to massage his throbbing temples. "If you're not willing to talk to me, then I can do nothing to make things better for you. You're on break for the rest of the day." He handed her the umbrella and turned to leave, rain be damned.

"It's my father," she whispered.

William looked over his shoulder at her. "What about your father?"

The dossier he'd glossed over had portrayed Reginald Roth as a successful entrepreneur in the prime of his life. He was in peak condition, signing deals and shaking hands across Europe to further Roth Enterprises.

"He's sick." Claudette's eyes welled with tears. "He's got a rare form of leukemia, only diagnosed a few months ago. It's absolutely ravaging him. He's on constant chemotherapy."

William moved in close and ducked his head to get under the umbrella. "How has he kept this from the press?"

"A body double," Claudette said resignedly. "Devon has been my father's bodyguard for years, and he's doubled for him on more than one occasion. With some effort on his part and a talented makeup artist who knows how to keep his mouth shut, Devon can pass for my father from afar or with people who don't know him well."

"Ah." It made sense that a man like her father wouldn't want news of his illness to get out. "And what does this sickness have to do with you rushing through your training?"

"My father is going in for surgery at the end of the month," she replied. "And so am I."

William frowned. "What are you talking about?"

"He needs a bone-marrow transplant," she said. "I'm the closest match."

Of course she was. And damn her for only telling him this now. "That would be the 'week in Nice' you've had on your schedule, then," he said.

"Yes." Claudette pressed a hand to her eyes, dashing a few tears away. "It would all have worked out fine if I hadn't gotten ambitious and decided to break into Clarence House. My mother has always fancied that particular tiara, and I thought it would be a nice gift for her. She's been so upset over the cancer, far more than my father, and I was going to tell her it was a replica."

"While actually gifting her the Queen Consort's real crown."

Claudette shrugged, and there was the ghost of a smile on her face. "You have to admit that it would make an excellent present."

William didn't have to admit anything, even though

privately he admired her gutsiness. He'd done his fair share of pushing back the weight of the world by doubling down on work. That she did the same wasn't surprising, but the timing was unfortunate. "Can your father delay the surgery?"

Claudette bit her lower lip. "No. He's already put it off to the point where his doctors worry his recovery could be affected. This is his best chance, and I'm the best donor."

"You won't make much of a donor at all if you're killed in Volkov's mansion."

"I'll get it right next time! Just let me try again, and—"

"No." Her face fell, but William kept speaking. "You've already worked too hard today. After supper—which Mrs. Wainwright tells me is your favorite, by the way—we'll go over the extraction plan again. Tomorrow, you can start fresh on the infiltration, and if you dedicate yourself to my schedule and make the kind of progress I know you're capable of, I'll do everything I can to move the heist forward."

It wasn't going to be easy.

They'd synced their break-in with a major technology show in Moscow, one that Volkov was sure to be in town for. He hosted events in his mansion almost every night while he was around, but there was no telling when precisely he would arrive, and some events would be easier to infiltrate than others.

"Thank you." She looked at him as if he were her hero, and he liked her looking at him like that too much.

"I can't promise anything," William warned. "The one thing I won't compromise on is your safety."

"I know." Claudette smiled gently. "And I appreciate it, but mine is not the only life on the line. My father is running out of time."

In the rain, with the fog rolling around them, she looked ethereal, and the urge to pull her close and hold her tight was overwhelming. He wanted to shield her and protect her from sorrow as well as from bullets and angry oligarchs.

Hell, he wanted to share a bottle of wine with her over a five-course meal and talk to her about things other than blind spots, lasers, and listening devices.

Most of all, he wanted her in his bed, under him and over him, with her beautiful face free of worry and stress, happy because she was with him.

It was a nice dream and would remain just that—a wishful fantasy of a life neither of them would ever have.

They were both adrenaline junkies, and people like them didn't get a happy ending.

"I'll do my best to get you to the hospital on time."

"You're kinder than I'd hoped," Claudette said. "I'm sorry about giving you so much trouble."

Trying to conceal the momentary melancholy he'd allowed himself to indulge in, William snorted. "You're nothing compared to some of the people I've been saddled with. Trust me, as long as the house isn't on fire, you're not the worst. In fact, you are pretty impressive." He held out his arm. "Shall we go back? I was quite serious about that supper."

"I would love to." She slipped her hand into his elbow. "Thank you. I—oh!" Claudette pulled the wrapped napkin out of the pocket of William's raincoat. "What's this?"

"Something Mrs. Wainwright said you'd like."

She opened up the napkin and revealed two chocolate crackle biscuits. "Mm," she hummed, inhaling the rich scent. "These were my favorite when I was a kid." After a second, she held the napkin out to William. "Would you like one?"

I'll take whatever you're in the mood to give me. He accepted a cookie and bit into it. It was still warm in the center, kind of like how he felt right now.

Walking arm in arm in comfortable silence, they headed back to the mansion, and it felt too bloody good.

If he didn't start putting more distance between them, he would be majorly screwed.

William couldn't let himself fall for any woman, let alone a woman like Claudette Roth.

They lived in different worlds, and as soon as this mission was over, she would be back to the dazzling land of money and glamour, while he would be sent on another undercover assignment.

For all he knew, he could be impersonating an arms dealer in sub-Saharan Africa next month.

Besides, how presumptuous was he to think she would even want him?

19

CLAUDETTE

"Are you ready?"

Claudette clenched her hands into fists and then shook them out. This was it—her final run-through before the actual mission. She'd gone over the various sections of this course what felt like a hundred times over the past three weeks, and she'd performed them all flawlessly…in parts.

This was all of it put together at last: full tilt, no breaks, no stops.

A dress rehearsal, as it was called in theater circles, just with a deadlier stage. If she didn't get it right, the repercussions wouldn't be boos.

They might come in the form of bullets. The critical part of her mission was placing the listening device and the spyware where they wouldn't be found and without anyone suspecting her of anything other than theft. Once those were in place and active, it was acceptable for her to get caught.

Well, acceptable to William and his handlers, but not to Claudette. God only knew what Volkov would do to her.

The problem was that William's success might depend on her getting caught and creating the distraction he needed to complete his part of the mission.

The critical part of disabling the triggers.

After he was done with that, he could focus on rescuing her.

As terrifying as it seemed, she knew she could count on him. If the last week had taught her anything, it was that he would always have her back.

As she recalled their last shooting practice, heat coursed through her.

Claudette remembered the feel of William's strong hands and long fingers on hers vividly as he helped her stabilize her shooting stance—his body pressed close, the scent of his aftershave suffusing her senses, and the raw maleness of him scrambling her brain.

Had he done it on purpose to get her past her instinctive repulsion toward the weapon, so she could actually aim the damn thing?

Had he known the effect he would have on her? "Claudette?"

"Sorry," she said, blinking herself back into the present moment. "I'm ready."

"Glad to have you back." William sounded faintly amused. "For a moment there, you looked as if your body was here, but your mind was far away."

If he only knew that her mind hadn't been far at all. In fact, it had been dangerously close.

Claudette felt her cheeks warm up. "Are you done talking?"

"I am. Beginning in three…two…one…"

The ballroom door in front of her opened, and Claudette swept in to the sound of music. There were no people, but a bunch of Roombas darted across the floor, each labeled with its role. Claudette mimed taking a glass of champagne, swanned over toward the wall, and—oops! She dropped it—how clumsy of her… "Sir, no, please, let me just…."

She had the guard's keycard. Time to slip out into the hallway.

Avoiding the pressure plate, she pulled the tiny aerosol can out of her décolletage and sprayed the air. As the laser array lit up bright red, she quickly tied the long skirt of her evening gown to her legs to keep it from billowing out and touching the beams. She rolled, flipped, and jumped through the grid of laser lights, finally ending up outside the office door.

Ha, let's see William or any of the other male agents doing that in ten seconds flat and in high heels.

Easy, easy…

One quick snip and she was in. Computer—there, turn it on—and spyware installed. Perfect. Now the listening device…and done.

Now came the fun part—getting to the Fabergé eggs.

Volkov had a private art gallery attached to his bedroom—naturally.

Claudette wondered how often the women he courted

were taken to that gallery and shuttled from one spot to the next, depending on what they found more interesting.

Down the hall a bit further, second door on the right...this one had a palm reader, but thanks to a special request from William to MI6's tech lab, Claudette was wearing a glove that was an exact replica of Volkov's right palm. She pressed it to the reader, which briefly glowed green, then let her in. Lovely.

Of course, there were no actual art pieces here, but rather representations of the art itself in cutout form on various plinths and walls. Claudette admired a Caravaggio and glanced at a Monet before focusing on the eggs. God, she was a bit of a cliché when it came to her preferred targets, but there was something undeniably appealing about the luster of gold and gems. She stepped in front of the display, picked her target, and—

Beepbeepbeepbeep! There was the alarm, set off just like she'd intended.

Now she could either wait to be caught or...

Claudette bit her lower lip for a moment. What the hell. She ripped off most of the lower part of her skirt, fashioned it quickly into a bag, and stuffed the imitation egg into it. Tying it around her chest, she then booked it for the door.

William laughed over the earpiece. "Bold move. You think you can make it to the extraction point?"

Claudette's mouth curled into a smile. "I'm certainly going to try."

"It won't be easy."

"Good." She slipped out of the room, turned, and ran toward the windows at the end of the hall.

She wasn't a good shot, but shooting out a window didn't require much accuracy.

However, hitting the cameras watching her from the corners of the hall was more of a challenge. She couldn't hit them while running. She knew that much about her own capabilities.

Claudette paused, took careful aim, and fired on the camera on the right.

Her practice gun looked and weighed precisely like the real thing, but instead of bullets, it shot a signal that activated the sensor it hit, provided that it was close enough and that her aim was true.

As the red light beneath the camera winked out, she turned and shot the second one on the left.

Missed, damn it.

She fired again. The light vanished.

Ha! Now to take out the window.

Claudette aimed and fired. The glass slid to the side—obviously, they weren't going to replace the window every time the simulation was run.

As she sprinted back and hid in the office, the doors at the end of the hallway opened, and the sound of zooming machines rushed by—the Roomba guards.

Given the little setup she'd prepared, the guards should assume she'd gone through the window. That should give her the time she needed to sneak back into the ballroom and leave via the side door.

Claudette was about to push the office door open when she detected a new sound—heavy footsteps stalking down the hall outside. She froze, barely breathing as she waited for them to move on. Her heart raced more than was reasonable.

Real as it was, this was still just a simulation.

It was probably William, or possibly Jenkins the groundskeeper, or even Mrs. Wainwright, both MI6 pensioners and no threat to her, but the footsteps added a sense of reality to the simulation, making them sound menacing.

As the sound of footsteps faded, Claudette rearranged the cloth containing the fake egg and shoved it beneath her remaining skirt, giving it more of a retro, puffed-up look.

Slipping out of the office, she ran toward the ballroom with no regard for the laser arrays or the pressure plates.

The alarm had been set off, the dogs were loose, and all she had to do now was outsmart the guards and get to the rendezvous point.

20

CLAUDETTE

As two sharp cracks sounded behind Claudette, she didn't panic until the wooden molding around the door in front of her cracked and shredded.

What the hell?

Why were they using real bullets in a simulation?

Could Volkov have discovered their mission and launched a preemptive strike?

No, that didn't make any sense.

This was still a simulation, and they were testing her response under fire, literally.

With her legs shaking and her heart thundering in her chest, she barely managed to get the door open and slip back into the ballroom.

It was tempting to rush through and ignore the imitation crowd,

She was being shot at! For real! No time for swanning through the Roombas.

What was she supposed to do if this was for real?

She had to stick with the plan.

If she broke under fire and fled, she would alert every person in the simulation ballroom to the fact that she was a thief on the run. If that were for real, she would blow the mission.

She had to keep going.

Slow, steady—don't let them know you're rattled. Nothing is wrong.

Everything is fine.

Years of experience had taught Claudette to fake fine with the best of them.

She didn't turn or look to see if anyone was coming after her. She made her way through the ballroom like she hadn't just reappeared there, pausing and mingling where imitation guests had gathered until she was close enough to an exit to take advantage of it.

Pulling out her keycard, she gave it a swipe and slipped out into the servants' hallway. Right would lead to the kitchen, left would take her to the mudroom and outside.

She went left, got to the door, and let herself out into the chill night air. As goosebumps rippled across her bare arms, she gave in to the urge to hug herself.

There. Now all she had to do was—

An iron grip clasped her around the chest, locking her arms in place before her. Claudette shrieked and smashed her head backward in an effort to hit her attacker in the face. She missed—with her head, but the heel she kicked back into the man's groin struck hard.

He groaned and bent forward far enough that a hard strike back with her hips was enough to dislodge him. She began to run—and found her leg grabbed and lifted into the air, taking her off her feet.

Claudette hit the ground flat on her back, gun already pulled, and fired a round into his chest.

Bang!

A buzzer sounded somewhere on the masked man's body.

A second later, he pulled the balaclava off his face, and... even knowing she should expect William, it was still a rush of relief to see him looking down at her, grinning fiercely.

"Not bad." He extended a hand to her.

As Claudette took it, William hoisted her up so forcefully that she fell forward against him. Splaying her hands across his chest, she was disappointed to feel a padded vest instead of the enticing contours of his body.

She could imagine them, though.

She'd been spending a lot of time lately imagining how he looked beneath his clothes...

Not the right time, girl.

"How did that kick not leave you gagging?" she asked instead.

She ought to step back, but he hadn't said anything yet and was so delightfully warm.

Yes. Warm. That was why she was clinging to him so fiercely.

"Groin protector." He tapped his lower abdomen. "It goes up my spine and further than my hips in the front. Helps dissipate the force."

Claudette arched an eyebrow. "How many women have tried to kick you in the balls?"

"Enough to teach me to take precautions." He relaxed his grip on her but didn't let go. "So, this run was interesting."

Oh God, here it comes.

Her final assessment. And it didn't sound like it was off to a good start.

Claudette pulled back, immediately missing William's heat but not willing to make herself vulnerable while he sealed her fate and possibly the fate of her father along with it.

"I did my best," she said, lifting her chin high. "If that's not good enough for you, then—"

"I didn't say it wasn't good enough."

Wait...what?

"Then why not just tell me that I've passed?"

"Where would the fun be in that?" He laughed as Claudette smacked him on the shoulder. "No, I'm sorry, but really, you did an excellent job. You kept your head, and you improvised. Both are essential in the field, but the ability to improvise separates a great operative from just a good one." He put his hand on her shoulder. "You'll need both on this mission." He grinned. "We are heading out."

Claudette gripped his forearm. "You've found a chance for us to get in?"

Given the situation with her father, timing was the true bugbear of this assignment. She'd known that William would try, but she hadn't really believed that he would come through for her.

"I have, but it's going to be more difficult for you than what we originally planned. Instead of infiltrating the large gathering of people Volkov will be entertaining later this month, we will take advantage of a smaller gathering he's hosting this week to showcase his collection to a small group of art lovers. The problem won't be getting you in. It will be you sneaking away for long enough to get into his office."

That was indeed a serious problem, especially given Claudette's jewel-thief cover, but she had to do it. Her father's surgery was in eight days, and he was counting on her to be there.

She couldn't let him down, not when his life was on the line.

And she wasn't going to let William down either.

"I'll make it work," she vowed.

"We will make it work," he said. "I'll be there with you, and it's my responsibility to get you through this." He looked into her eyes. "I take that job very seriously."

That's not your only job.

It wasn't the chill in the air that made Claudette suddenly shiver. William's most important job would be handling the nuclear triggers. She wasn't sure how and didn't really want to know either. The point was, William's promise could only go so far.

"Claudette?"

She realized that she'd zoned out and refocused on him with a smile. "Sorry. I'm starting to get quite cold."

"Of course." He slid an arm around her.

Claudette couldn't help but lean further into William. Being close to him felt so good, so right. She shut her eyes for a moment, reveling in the contact. She'd never known a man like him before, someone who respected her for her talents instead of coveting her for her wealth and beauty.

She only wished she'd met him under different circumstances.

"Let's get inside," he continued, guiding them back into the manor house. "We'll debrief, then pack up. We've got to be in Moscow by mid-afternoon tomorrow."

Claudette nodded. "I'm ready."

Well, as ready as she possibly could be. Hopefully, it was enough.

21

WILLIAM

Before tonight, William had never truly appreciated just how much preparation a woman had to undergo to put on her suit of social armor. Watching Claudette get ready for the intimate gathering he'd secured her an invitation to, he found that he both loved and hated to see the transformation she was undergoing.

He had been spoiled by three weeks spent with the real Claudette. She'd had no reason to hide any part of herself from him, save perhaps for her vulnerability, but in the end, she'd shown him that as well.

He admired her dedication to her father.

Not that he would have done things differently if he were in her shoes, but many people would have crumbled under pressure and given up.

Not Claudette, though. She was a fierce fighter and one of the best operatives he'd ever had the pleasure of training.

A real talent that should be utilized for better things than stealing jewels.

William was amazed by everything Claudette had mastered in such a short time, and so taken with the woman herself that he'd forgotten there was more to her than what he'd seen during training.

That side, that personal, intimate side of her, was methodically covered and concealed as she readied herself for Volkov's party.

Away went the straight-shouldered confidence, replaced with a breezy waifishness that gave her the slightest of slouches even in high heels. Gone were her straightforward smiles, replaced by giggling grins and girlish hair flips. Her makeup artfully enlarged her eyes and drew attention to her lips, while her necklace, taken from her personal jewelry collection, plunged so low that it practically vanished in her cleavage. Her dress was a vivid, off-the-shoulder work of art, whose ruffled skirt had been modified by Mrs. Wainwright to contain pouches for various treasures and to hold the thumb drive that contained the spyware. The only other thing they'd modified for her was the massive emerald earrings, which acted as a communicator and GPS locator.

As William neared Volkov's property, he glanced through the rearview mirror at the stunning woman sitting in the back of the limousine, and those earrings caught his eye, but not in a good way. It occurred to him that the designers had overdone it. The earrings were too big for Claudette's delicate face and not as elegant as the rest of her jewelry.

Volkov might take notice, but it was too late to do anything about them.

"You okay back there?" he asked.

She nodded, the massive earrings swinging. "Let's do this."

He turned into the lane leading to Volkov's mansion.

Like all other houses in the upmarket Moscow neighborhood, Volkov's property was fenced off, its grounds so extensive that the house wasn't visible from the street.

Keeping his cap low, William pulled up to the gate where an armed guard was stationed inside a small hut.

The guard came out to meet them, one hand on his sidearm. He smiled politely as William rolled down the window. *"Dobryy vecher."*

"Wait, sorry, wait!" Claudette rolled down the back passenger window and leaned out. "I'm so sorry, but my Russian's a little...nonexistent." She batted her eyelashes at the guard. "I'm here for the party."

"Name and invitation, please," the guard said with a perfect English accent.

Claudette handed over the garish, gold-leafed card William had obtained for her. "Claudette Roth," she said. "Plus my driver, Leon...something or other."

The guard inspected the invitation, pulled out his phone, took a picture of Claudette, pressed send, and then waited.

As a minute passed and then another, Claudette began to squirm in the back seat, her smile giving way to a pout.

"I swear, I'm on the guest list!" she whined. "Greggy knows my father! Call him—no, let me call him, I'll—"

The guard's phone beeped. "Your invitation and identity

have been verified, Miss Roth," he said, then glanced at William. "After your driver drops you off at the main house, he'll have to wait outside the grounds until you're ready to be picked up."

She waved a hand. "That's no problem. He's got Netflix."

William waited for the guard to walk away and the gate to retract before turning back and raising an eyebrow at her. "Netflix?"

Claudette shrugged.

"It's the perfect way for a bored chauffeur to pass the time while waiting for his spoiled charge. That's what my father's driver does when waiting for him to be done with his meetings." Her chin wobbled a little.

William didn't respond. Any show of empathy would divert her attention from what she was about to do, or worse, make her tear up and ruin her makeup.

Now was not the time to think about her father's situation.

As the private road curved and the well-lit home came into view, Claudette sucked in a breath. "It doesn't look anything like where we practiced."

"It's only different on the outside. The inside will be similar enough. Trust me."

"I do," she murmured. "I trust you."

When William pulled up in front of Volkov's mansion, half a dozen people were outside, either in the process of exiting their cars or greeting the guests.

One of them was Volkov, easily identified by his salt-and-pepper beard, which trailed all the way down to his prodigious belly and made him look like a very well-dressed

Santa Claus. His kindly smile while greeting his guests only added to the illusion.

How deceptive appearances could be.

"You won't be able to hear my voice," William said softly as he brought the car to a stop. "But I'll be able to hear what you and everyone around you say. Protect yourself at all times. No matter where they put you, I'll come for you as soon as I secure the triggers."

Or rather, the chips that controlled the triggers.

The nuclear triggers were too large for one man to carry out alone. Instead, he was going to locate the bunker where the triggers were being kept and pry out their control chips. Without them, the nuclear warheads would be good for nothing but lobbing in the general direction of an enemy and hoping they blew up at the right time.

It was precise work that had to be done quickly, and splitting his attention between his mission and Claudette would be challenging, but he couldn't imagine doing this any other way.

She took a bracing breath, nodded, and then turned a brilliant, empty smile on him. It was perfect, and perfectly chilling to see such a blank expression on her face. "I'll be fine, of course," she said.

William stepped out of the car, opened the back passenger door, and offered Claudette a hand.

She picked up her clutch and took his hand. "Thank you, Leon. I'll call you when I'm ready to leave."

He nodded. "Enjoy your evening, Miss Roth."

William watched Claudette walk to the front of the

mansion, seemingly immune to the cold, elegant with a hint of youthful bounce in her gait.

She greeted Volkov as if he were an old friend, and he seemed instantly charmed by her, but when the old lecher raised her hand to his filthy mouth and pressed a kiss against her knuckles, unexpected rage washed over William.

When she giggled, bile rose in his throat.

He had to get out of there before he ruined his cover by pistol-whipping that bastard across the face. Forcing himself to turn around without giving Claudette another look, William got back behind the wheel and pulled out onto the pink gravel path.

22

WILLIAM

The cameras hidden in the car's frame were doing their job, zooming in on anything and everything within range and correlating it to the maps the agents in charge of this mission had already collected and programmed into the database—personnel, building placement, and local flora updated.

"Are you out the gate?" Liam asked through the earpiece in William's left ear.

In the right one, William could hear Claudette making nice with the other guests. The booming bass notes of Volkov's voice in the background were grating on his nerves. The scumbag was staying close to her so far, which could be problematic.

"Will?" Liam said. "Are you there?"

"Sorry," he said as the gate opened for him. "Out of the gate."

Driving away from the guard and his suspicious gaze,

William didn't veer into a side road until he was well out of sight of the manor and its staff.

"You're allowing yourself to get distracted by what's going on with Claudette. Do I need to cut the feed from her earpiece?"

William's hands tightened on the wheel. "Don't you dare," he said vehemently, surprising himself.

"Then remember the order of operations here, Agent Kentworth. No matter what is going on with Miss Roth, your first priority is decommissioning those nuclear triggers."

"Understood."

"Then it's time to get to work."

Yes, it was.

William recalibrated his focus to the mission ahead.

There was nothing quite like a good infiltration. He never allowed himself to become overconfident, which was a folly of rookies, but it wasn't an exaggeration to say that he was one of the best operatives MI6 had, especially when completing solo missions. Whether he had to work his way through a crowd or kill his way across an enemy stronghold, William had honed his senses to the point that the challenges in front of him were just that—challenges.

No situation was ever hopeless, not even one like this, where the triggers were in a bunker guarded by three men in the middle of a rich sociopath's private estate. There were roving patrols, infrared cameras, dogs, and who knew what else.

Child's play.

In times like this, William likened himself to a conduit, a vessel dedicated to nothing but the mission.

Following the instructions given to him by his handler, he took cover, darted forward, took careful shots, and laid a hidden trail of mayhem behind him to be triggered on his way out.

Keeping a state of Zen, he was an unfeeling machine—a weapon—honed and sharpened by relentless training. He didn't feel fear. He didn't feel empathy. He did his job.

Except, his mission wasn't solo this time, and although he wasn't afraid for himself, he was terrified for Claudette. Every minute she spent inside that mansion, he grew increasingly fearful for her.

"I think you'll like seeing these," Volkov purred close to her ear—so close that the sound crackled over the microphone. "They're a poor substitute for having a beautiful woman like yourself in my home, but they glitter quite nicely."

Claudette laughed. "I'm sure I'll adore them! Nothing is quite so exquisitely tempting as a Fabergé egg, is it?"

"Oh, I can think of something," Volkov drawled.

As Claudette squealed with a shock of laughter, William shot the next guard straight through the head.

"Feedback!" Liam hissed with a note of warning.

"Another one down."

Liam was right to be angry. William shouldn't have shot the guard from a distance.

"Shut his radio transmitter off now!" Liam barked into his ear.

William raced over to the dead man's body, yanked the

helmet off his head, and shut down the internal radio, but not before he heard a concerned voice asking in Russian what that noise had been.

"That was poorly executed, Agent Kentworth," Liam chided. "Get it together. You're almost there."

William didn't need Liam to point it out to him. He was angry at himself for not taking out the guard silently, and endangering the entire mission because his head wasn't where it was supposed to be.

Keeping Claudette safe meant taking out every person who might send an emergency message to Volkov, but he needed to be smart about it and do it as stealthily as possible. Two more guards were standing outside the entrance to the bunker, and this time, William got close and personal with the kills.

It had been odd doing that while Claudette trilled in his ear, drinking champagne and clattering along in her heels as Volkov led his guests to the art gallery.

The mission had changed so much from what they'd practiced that he feared she wouldn't be able to pull it off, especially with the sticky Russian billionaire refusing to budge from her side.

William hoisted one of the guard's bodies up to the scanner and pried his eye open for the retinal authentication. As the heavy door swung open, he stepped into the darkened corridor and headed toward the repository at the end of it. In his ear, he heard Claudette chat with Volkov as they waltzed to the sound of the quartet playing in the background.

Were the Russian's filthy hands crawling down the back of her sexy green dress? Was he going to—

Blam, blam, blam!

Three shots straight to the fucking chest.

Damn it all to hell.

William went down. There was no hope of him keeping his feet, not against that sort of impact, but he managed to lob a smoke grenade right after he'd hit the floor.

He should have done that the second he'd started down this corridor. He knew that there were cameras inside and a third man. Of bloody course he had known that, but once again, his head had been with Claudette instead of where it should have been.

More gunfire came from the end of the hall, but the shooter was firing blind, hitting the wall over William's head.

"Will! Talk to me! What's going on?"

"Little busy at the moment," he grunted as he rolled to the side.

The shooter was being methodical now. No longer spraying bullets indiscriminately, he was shooting in a grid pattern, going from top to bottom. He would hit William in another few seconds.

The Kevlar vest was good, but it didn't cover his entire body. Extrapolating as best he could from the ground, William fired in the direction of the shooter. His magazine was almost empty at this point, and he had only one more.

Who would run out of ammunition first? He or the shooter? That wasn't how his life was going to end. It couldn't. Claudette was counting on him to save her.

His penultimate shot corresponded with an abrupt halt in return fire, and as he hastily swapped out the spent magazine for another, he lay low and held his breath.

Thud.

The smoke dissipated enough for him to see the body suddenly slouch onto the floor.

He'd gotten him.

Shit, that had been close.

"Are you there?" Liam sounded alarmed.

The guy had often sounded worried, but this was the first time in a long time William could actually recall him sounding frantic.

"Are you fucking alive? Answer me!"

"I'm here," William grunted, rolling over onto his side and getting to his feet. His ribs ached, both from the impact of the bullets and the fall he'd taken to the concrete floor. He inhaled and winced—yeah, that one might be cracked. "I'm fine."

"Of course you are," Liam said acridly, but there was relief there too. "What the hell happened?"

"Let's save the interrogation for when I'm done with the job, all right?" Which needed to be soon.

William continued down the hall, pulling the body of the fallen guard with him and using his retina to open the door at the back.

He found the triggers. "I'm in."

"Hallelujah," Liam said. "And now it is time for the interrogation. You got distracted, didn't you?"

Not deigning to reply, William took out his tools.

His silence was apparently answer enough. "I told you

not to listen to Miss Roth while you're working. Get your priorities straight, Agent Kentworth."

"They're straight," William murmured as he unscrewed the plate protecting the computer interface. There, now he just had to... "I'm here, aren't I?"

And...done.

He smiled as he tucked the chip away in his pocket, then moved on to the next. One down, nine to go.

Liam chuckled in his ear. "Without me making sure that you followed the directives of the mission, you would be monitoring her with a set of binoculars from a tree somewhere like a schoolboy spying on his crush."

"Is that how you did courting back in the day?" William said absently, his ear still tuned to Claudette. "Frankly, that sounds rather creepy."

The lack of music in the background indicated that the dancing part of the evening had wound down. Given the oohs and aahs, the guests had moved on to the gallery itself.

Two triggers down. Eight to go.

"What do you think?" Volkov's voice was louder than it should have been, which meant that his mouth was too close to her ear again.

William fought the urge to grind his teeth.

"Exquisite," Claudette said breathily. "I've never seen its like before! The artist was truly exceptional."

"Indeed. See the way that tendril of gold curls just so...."

"Oh!" Claudette laughed again, but William knew her well enough to hear the undercurrent of genuine discomfort beneath it. "Greggy, honestly, we've only just met! And there are all these people around, surely you don't want to make a spectacle."

"You would make the finest spectacle I've ever seen," the Russian growled possessively. As if he had any right to her, that son of a—

Three down. Seven to go.

"Well, you're not wrong," Claudette giggled. "But honestly, all these people...I just can't. I'm not comfortable like this. I...if you really want me to," her voice lowered, "then perhaps it's best if I stay the night."

"Is it now?" Volkov sounded pleased.

"I'd like to." She made a delighted humming sound. "So, in the meantime, don't neglect the rest of your guests. I'm not going anywhere."

"I'll hold you to that."

"I'm sure you will."

There was that worry again. She was about to make her move, and William wasn't done with the triggers yet.

Four down. Six to go.

William worked as fast as he could, listening to Claudette extricate herself from Volkov's tenacious grasp and excuse herself from the rest of the group to go powder her nose.

"I'm getting his handprint in place," she whispered as she walked down the hall.

He couldn't hear the clacking sound of her heels, which meant that she'd taken them off.

"Heading to his office now...it worked!" The triumph in her voice was clear. "Give me a moment." There were shuffling sounds and a few drawers being opened. "I've got his computer. Turning it on and uploading the spyware."

Five down. Five to go.

"It's uploading. I'm going to pick a spot for the bug. Hmm. This is the most hideous lamp I've ever seen, but it's brass. Lovely, nice and heavy, let's put it…here. The upload is done. Removing the thumb drive. Now I just need to get back to the party. It should be simple for me to—"

"*Ruki vverkh!*" The command startled William.

Bloody hell. He'd been so intent on finishing up the chips so he could get to Claudette that he'd completely missed the entrance of a new group of guards. "Agent Kentworth," Liam said crisply over the earpiece. "Your prime objective is to complete this mission. Use any means necessary to destroy those chips. Extricating yourself is secondary, and Miss Roth is of no consequence to us."

Damn and blast. William ground his teeth as he turned to face his attackers.

This was about to get messy.

23

CLAUDETTE

"I'm back." Claudette sauntered over to Volkov. "All freshened up." She puckered her lips, which were sporting a new coat of red lipstick.

She'd been gone all of ten minutes, a perfectly acceptable time for a woman to spend powdering her nose.

"Excellent." He laughed as he drew her close to his side, one heavy arm clenched around her waist like a vise. "It's good of you to keep yourself fresh for me, eh?" He continued to the next Fabergé egg. "I like a woman who puts effort into looking beautiful for her man."

Claudette smiled aimlessly and directed her attention to the egg. If she wasn't looking at something else, the urge to shudder and pull away from Volkov might overwhelm her. At least the eggs were beautiful and didn't stink of harsh tobacco and black tea. This one was particularly lovely, an egg shaped like a carriage with a polished blue enamel shell and gold accents. The wheels were twists of spiraled gold, the tiny windows had gold frames, and within the egg itself sat two figures, a man and a woman, locked in a passionate embrace.

Cinderella and her prince.

"Romantic, isn't it?" Volkov whispered in her ear, his breath moist. "You know, I could arrange to—" He stopped as his pocket buzzed and pulled out his phone with a curse. "*Da?*" he barked.

Claudette was close enough to hear the frantic conversation coming through, her knowledge of Russian just barely good enough to understand every third word or so, but it was enough to get the gist of what was going on.

Something about an intruder and needing support.

William had been busy, and he'd been discovered, but if they were asking for support, they didn't have him yet.

That was good, right?

Volkov's face got darker with every word the guy on the other side was saying. He told the man to wait, then ended the call and turned to his guests.

"I'm afraid I have to end our party early," he said coldly, all his previous affability gone. "For your own safety, I must insist that you all leave at once."

Everyone in the room knew better than to ask what was going on or express disappointment over the abrupt ending of the party. With understanding murmurs and bowed heads, they briskly made their way out of the gallery and down the hall.

As Claudette watched them go, her heart was beating so fast that it was a wonder Volkov didn't hear it.

Was there any way she could help William?

All this time, they'd made plans for what to do when

Claudette was found out: where she would likely be taken, how he would rescue her, and what she might do if he was late. They had never talked about what would happen if he was the one who got found out first.

She realized now what an enormous oversight that had been.

"You need to leave, my sweet." Volkov smiled with regret in his beady eyes. Letting go of her waist, he took a step back. "Call your driver."

This was her best chance to get out of there. She wouldn't be able to call William to get her, but surely she could get a ride with one of the other guests. Undoubtedly, Grable had told William to cut his losses and leave her here. She knew the handler didn't prioritize her safety, especially not over William's. He would tell William to go and let her figure out her own escape.

And if William was dead, no one would save her.

The thought chilled Claudette to the bone, and not because she feared what would happen to her.

She had a split second to decide—either stay and attempt to help William or leave and help herself. In the end, there was only one choice she could make.

"I can't call my driver." Assuming a coquettish expression, she stepped back into Volkov's reach. "He's the one distracting your men."

The arms dealer's eyes flared with anger, and his mouth twisted beneath his beard. "What is this?"

Claudette didn't let that stop her. "I told him to make a nuisance of himself," she continued, "because I came here tonight to rob you." She lowered her eyes and bit on her bottom lip. "I just couldn't help myself. I'm obsessed with Fabergé eggs, and you have so many. Surely you could part with one."

"You are insane," Volkov ground out, grabbing her by the arm and jerking her in close. "I've heard the rumors about you but didn't believe them." His eyes narrowed at her. "You're a fine piece of ass, and it would be a shame to kill you, but no one steals from me and lives."

Despite how tightly he was gripping her, Claudette forced herself not to wince.

"Wouldn't you rather fuck me instead?" she asked breathily.

Volkov paused. "What?"

"I don't steal for the money. I have all the money I'll ever need. I do it for the rush it gives me. Stealing from you gave me an incredible adrenaline rush, but after meeting you in person and being exposed to your commanding personality, all I could think about was getting you to take me to your bed." She pressed her free hand to his cheek. "You're the most dangerous, exciting man I have ever met." She leaned closer and whispered in his ear, "You have no idea how wet I am for you."

His grip on her arm slackened. "You are?"

"Oh, yes," Claudette lied, pulling her arm free only to drape them both over his shoulders. "I want you so badly that I ache. Take me to bed and make me yours."

She sounded like an actress in a bad porno movie, but Volkov was eating up every word. Men were idiots when it came to attractive women and their dicks.

Backing up her empty words would be a challenge, but

she would do everything in her power to save William, even if it meant letting the vile arms dealer touch her.

Her resolve was tested as Volkov dragged her into a kiss. His mouth tasted like foul cigarettes and fine wine, and his tie pin pressed harshly into her abdomen. He kissed like an animal, and when she couldn't hold back a shudder, she hoped he'd attribute it to desire.

When his phone went off again, he pulled it out with a grimace. Claudette ran her fingers down the buttons of his shirt as he shouted down the line.

"Just take care of it," he said in English for her sake. "I don't care what he did. The man is not important. Detain him, and don't bother me again for the rest of the night!" He ended the call, then turned his smirk on Claudette. "They won't kill your man." She shrugged as if it meant nothing to her. "He's a hireling, nothing more. He has probably already taken off."

Please, let him have taken off.

24

CLAUDETTE

The way to Volkov's suite had gone past in a blur. Claudette couldn't even have said how long it had taken to get there, only that it seemed too long of a trek and, at the same time, had come to an end far, far too soon.

She should have been taking notes, memorized the route to his private quarters, counted the guards, and taken note of the security cameras.

She hadn't managed any of that. Her mind was frozen in a state of shock, paralyzed with fear over what she'd thrown herself into. She wasn't a proper spy and had no idea how to fight off a man once she was in bed with him.

And how could she fight back, when she still wasn't sure if William was alive?

No, she was going to have to...

When he shoved her down onto the bed, Claudette let out a little shriek that was utterly unfeigned.

Volkov laughed. "You like it rough, eh?" He undid his tie

and threw it to the side along with the diamond tie pin he'd ground into her moments earlier. "Beautiful girls like you have their natural instincts stifled by high society. You may be pampered and rich, but all you really want is to lie on your back and experience a real man between your thighs and not one of those chinless dogs that drool at your feet."

Claudette shivered, resisting the urge to close her eyes. Everything he'd said made her cringe inside, partly because he was right.

She usually hated the type of man she was exposed to in polite society, but Volkov was nowhere near what she really wanted.

I want William. Oh God, I want William, please, please…

One hand touching his crotch, Volkov got onto his knees on the end of the bed and placed a possessive hand on her ankle. If his hand kept trailing up her leg, he would find the tiny Beretta Pico attached with a holster to the top of her thigh. It took everything Claudette had not to reach for it right then and there.

"I'll give you the things you can't get from your regular life," he boasted. "I'll show you how a real man handles a woman like you." The look on his face was half eagerness, half disdain. "You'll be lucky if you're able to walk in the morning, *koshechka*."

No, no, no, I can't do this, I can't.

Claudette held her breath as Volkov lowered himself onto her, knowing that the next time she opened her mouth, it would be to scream. She couldn't shoot Volkov, that would ruin the mission, but as soon as she could get her hands in between them, she would go for his eyes. If she could get him to rear back and then kick him in the head just right, she might be able to knock him out and buy both herself and William some time.

As his mouth pressed hungrily to her neck, Claudette spasmed and squeezed her eyes shut, readying herself to fight—

When Volkov's eager weight became dead weight, she gasped and scrambled out from under him as quickly as she could.

Was he dead? Perhaps she'd gotten incredibly lucky, and he'd suffered a sudden heart attack?

"Don't worry, I didn't kill him," a male's voice said.

"William!" Claudette jumped off the bed and ran over to where William stood at the foot of it, his gun in one hand, the other pressed lightly to his side. She threw herself into his arms, barely registering his grunt of pain as he held her close, his face pressed to her hair.

She exhaled what was almost a sob and just let herself breathe for a moment, deep, shuddering breaths of relief. "Good timing," she quipped, proud that her voice barely trembled.

"Are you all right?" William asked quietly.

"I'm fine. He didn't have time to...do anything."

"I heard it all," William said with an air of confession. He pulled back far enough to look into her eyes. "I've never wanted to hurt a man so much in all my life. I'm sorry it went as far as it did."

Claudette smiled. "It's all right. You're all right, so I'm all right."

The repetition seemed to loosen the fierce tension in William's body, and he even managed to smile back. "That's good because we're going to have to run from here on out."

Taking her hand, he led her to the door, then out into the hall. The mansion was strangely silent, but Claudette could hear sirens going off outside and the sound of men shouting to one another.

"What did you do?" she asked in surprise as he hustled them both down the hall and into a vast professional-grade kitchen.

William's mouth set in a grim line. "What I had to do to get to you."

Oh... For the first time, Claudette realized that William wasn't moving as fluidly as he normally did. His gait held a little limp, and his free hand was back to pressing his side.

"You're hurt," she murmured, feeling worried and guilty all at once.

"It's not so bad," he replied.

"Bollocks, it's not so bad!" She looked more closely at his face. "And where's your other earpiece?" The one he'd worn in his right ear was missing. It had been the one connecting him to his handler and the home office.

"Casualty of war."

"This isn't a wa—aa*h*!" A bullet ricocheted off one of the pots hanging from the ceiling just above their heads as they hurried down the aisle.

William turned in one smooth motion and fired on their assailant, getting him in the leg. His second shot took the falling man in the head.

Another attacker was right there behind him, though.

William fired once, then swore as his gun clicked over to empty. He dropped it, then swept his hand up the outside of Claudette's leg until he found the firearm secured to the top of her thigh.

Not even the sound of the man's body hitting the floor could detract from the thrill of excitement she felt in the wake of that particular move. Claudette opened her mouth to tell him as much when—

"Shit!" She pulled the closest pot down and chucked it straight at the man who'd just burst through the door they were heading for.

She got him right in the forehead, sending him over onto his back. Before he could recover, she ran over and kicked him as hard as she could right in the crotch.

"Good luck finding your balls after that," she announced as William came up from behind her.

She thought he was going to kill the retching man, but he just looked at her proudly. "Nice move."

"I've learned from the best," Claudette said as she flipped her hair over her shoulder. "Where are we headed?"

"The garage." William took her hand again and led her around the body.

They went through the door that the man she'd just taken down had come in through.

Sure enough, this was a garage, and it was a vast one. Two dozen cars of different makes and models sat there, lined up with precision, and—how fortunate, there was an entire section of the wall dedicated to housing their respective keys.

William looked over the cars, and a genuine grin brightened his handsome face. "I rather fancy the Koenigsegg for an afternoon drive, but tonight I'll take that bloody Rezvani Tank." He gestured toward the black, heavily armored SUV. "Let's get out of here, darling."

"Let's."

25

WILLIAM

William had been trained to drive practically anything and everything under the sun, but as he turned the Rezvani on, even he had to take a moment to marvel at the amenities this particular armored vehicle offered. Bulletproof glass and run-flat tires were standard, but this one also had thermal night vision and electrified door hinges to shock those unwary enough to try and pull them open to get to its passengers. Plus, it looked like Volkov had modified it to include some of his personal artillery stock.

Fucking perfect.

As vehicles went, he couldn't have hoped for a better one to protect his precious cargo, and he wasn't thinking about the damn computer chips.

Taking the Rezvani out of the garage and onto the gravel road, William activated the night vision and bright flares of light representing Volkov's men appeared on the screen. As he drove past them, bullets hit the sidewalls of the SUV, and Claudette inhaled sharply.

"They won't punch through," he promised. "Not even the armor-piercing ones. This car is a monster. They would need an RPG to do it some damage."

She cut him a sidelong glance with eyes as wide as saucers. "Then let's hope that they don't have rocket-propelled grenades."

He hoped so too.

After all, Volkov was an arms dealer, and his men might have weapons personal guards usually didn't carry.

Affecting a chuckle, he boasted with a confidence he didn't feel. "Even RPGs would barely scratch the paint on this tank. We were lucky to get it."

"Yeah." She slumped into the seat. "Lucky."

Evidently Claudette hadn't bought his act.

William bit back more reassurances and promises that he wanted to make. The truth was, they were still in a shitty situation. He'd barely been able to evade Volkov's men long enough to get to Claudette.

If they weren't a bunch of idiots incapable of independent thinking, and if their boss hadn't essentially left them floundering like chickens with their heads cut off, William could have been killed half a dozen times before reaching the mansion.

That he'd survived, he owed to Claudette and the sacrifice she'd been willing to commit to save his ass.

William didn't know how he could ever repay her for that, but first, he needed to get them out of there in one piece.

Volkov was still alive, and as soon as he regained his senses, he would whip his men into action. The Russian had been faintly groaning when they'd run from his bedroom, and he was a tough guy. It wouldn't take him long to take control of the situation.

Not killing him had been hard, and everything in William's soul had rebelled against leaving the scumbag alive, but if he'd killed the bastard, all the work Claudette had put into rigging the Russian's computer, and all the mortal danger they had both exposed themselves to would be for nothing.

Volkov needed to stay alive. For now. But his day would come.

The maggot had been about to rape Claudette, and for that, he would die at William's hands, slowly and excruciatingly. Glancing at her, he verified that her seatbelt was securely fastened and then deactivated the airbags. "Brace yourself. We're going to ram the gate."

As she gripped the oh-shit handle tight, William gunned the engine. Watching the speedometer rapidly rise, he felt the speed in the thrum of the engine and the crushing roll of the tires. More bullets came, but they were of no consequence. They couldn't penetrate the tank's body.

However, the massive metal gate they were about to smash through was a different matter.

The Rezvani was a beast, but it might not be powerful enough to break through the enormous gate.

The powerful impact was so jarring that the muscles in William's back spasmed, and the deafening noise of bending metal had his eardrums protest, but he kept his foot on the accelerator and the vehicle steady until the Rezvani broke through.

It dragged most of the gate behind them for nearly half a mile before it finally dropped off.

"Thank God." Claudette let go of the handle. "Are we going to be all right now?"

Even though William expected much more trouble before they were home free, he nodded. "Provided that we manage to make it to the extraction point." He looked her over. "Are you all right? Have you been hurt?"

She moved her head from side to side, stretching out her neck. "I'm fine." She frowned. "Why wouldn't we get to the extraction point?"

"Because we've just assaulted a politically ambitious Russian oligarch in his own home and killed his people. If he regained consciousness and is back on his feet, he's probably on the phone as we speak, contacting his buddies in the Kremlin. And if he's still out, then his chief of security is doing that for him."

"Right." Claudette let out a breath and pushed a strand of hair behind her ear. "I'm too shaken up to think straight."

"I bet."

She'd almost been raped tonight, had been shot at, and ramming the gate must have impacted her body as severely as it had his. It was a wonder she was holding it together as well as she was.

William glanced in the rearview mirror. No one yet, but that was only a temporary reprieve. "Couple that with the fact that this car is surely being tracked, and I'd say we're not out of the woods yet."

"Right," she said again. "So what do we do now?"

He glanced at her with a grin. "We'd better get deeper into the woods in a hurry, yeah?"

26

WILLIAM

The primary extraction point was fifteen miles to the north, on the outskirts of a park that spread into a wilderness area. Ideally, they'd be picked up there. If things didn't work out though, they'd retrieve their kit there and hike to the secondary extraction point, which would take days.

They were pushing the very edge of Claudette's deadline to help her father.

She relaxed against the black leather seat. "I put myself in your capable hands."

Was that a double entendre?

Was she trying to hint something, or was his imagination filling in the blanks that she hadn't actually left blank?

As William's mind conjured an image of his hands on her tight, round bottom, he hardened in an instant and had to discreetly adjust himself.

Talk about bad timing.

"Damn." She huffed out a breath.

Had she noticed him squirming in his seat? "What's the matter?"

A smirk lifted one corner of her lush lips. "I know that we didn't have time to revisit the gallery, but I would have liked to have lifted Volkov's Fabergé eggs while we were there." She sighed. "They were far too gorgeous for someone like him to own."

"Maybe next time," he joked.

Claudette smiled sadly and turned her face toward the window.

Oh, of course.

There would be no next time for her.

There would be no second mission, no deeper delve into the intersection of international arms dealing and global security, and no more high-profile infiltrations and daring heists.

As soon as they were done with this mission, Claudette would be whisked off to the hospital for the operation, and then she would return to the glamorous world of the monied elite—hopefully with some bodyguards, because after today she was going to have a Volkov-shaped target painted on her back.

William wondered if she'd considered that.

For some reason, it hadn't occurred to him before that Claudette would forever be in danger from the arms dealer. She hadn't entered the mission as a nameless operative who could disappear into obscurity.

She'd been recruited specifically for being a known name and having a particular reputation, and Liam had certainly been aware of the repercussions. But his handler didn't care what happened to Claudette once the mission objective had been achieved.

The only way to keep her safe was to go back and kill Volkov, but after the stunt William had pulled to rescue her from the oligarch, Liam would no doubt punish him for disobeying orders, and his next mission would probably be in Siberia.

He didn't regret going back for her, though. There had been nothing else he could have done.

Claudette had been in trouble because she'd chosen to help him instead of helping herself, and he couldn't repay her by leaving her behind.

Besides, he had gotten the bloody chips, so there was that.

"You're quiet." Claudette set her hand on his arm. "Is everything all right?"

He forced a smile. "Apart from the pressing need to put as much distance between us and Volkov's estate as possible, everything is perfectly fine."

She raised one eyebrow, silently calling him out on his bullshit.

William's heart rate accelerated as he considered telling her how he felt about her.

What could it hurt?

She would either reject him, and they would both move on unencumbered by this mission or...

As a trail of fire sped toward them, William responded reflexively before his brain could even engage. Twisting the wheel hard to the right, he sent the vehicle careening off the paved road and onto the greenway beside it, nearly crashing it into the trees.

A tree exploded behind them, pulling a startled gasp from Claudette's mouth. "What the hell?" She twisted around to look through the rear window.

A convoy of dark vehicles had materialized behind them, and as William forced the SUV back onto the road, he made out the silhouette of a man disappearing through the sunroof of one of the larger cars.

When he reappeared, he was holding what looked like a…

"Fuck!" William twisted the wheel hard to the left, and again, the handheld missile barely missed their vehicle.

He wouldn't be able to keep this up.

William couldn't outrun them, so his only choice was to take out the convoy.

Luckily, Volkov had equipped the Rezvani with offensive as well as defensive weapons.

If he could just figure out how to…

Ah, there.

The machine gun deployed at the front of the car. Now he just needed to get in a position to use it.

William spun the wheel one more time with more precise control than before. The heavy SUV skidded into a turn that nearly bowled it over onto its side, but William managed to keep it righted, and as soon as they were stable, he slammed on the gas, sending them careening back at the convoy.

"What are you—" Claudette screeched.

He found the command to fire and watched as the heavy

Gatling-style machine gun tore into the incoming vehicles. The one in front burst into flames and veered off the road, but the ones behind it managed to evade the first salvo.

"Damn it." He couldn't drive and fire at the same time. "Claudette, use this switch to control the gun's targeting."

She was a lousy shot, and it would have been better for her to drive and for him to shoot, but they didn't have time to switch.

"I'm on it." With a determined expression on her beautiful face, she took over control of the machine gun, shifting its aim at the cars that were trying to evade the fire.

Unbelievably, she managed to blow out the tires of the one on the right just before William drove them straight into the gap between the pursuing vehicles.

It was too narrow for them to pass through, but that was the whole point. The tank had a stability that the others didn't.

Bam! He nudged the car on the left.

The man in the passenger seat was able to get a few shots off with his pistol, but all he'd accomplished before his vehicle rolled off the road was dinging the SUV's windows.

William watched with satisfaction as they drove right into a tree, smashing the entire front of the vehicle like a tin can.

Excellent. He turned the wheel to right the tank and turn in the direction they needed to be heading. They were only three miles from the extraction point now, close enough to taste it.

He just had to outrun the Russian goons chasing them for a little bit longer, and—

"Look out!" Claudette screamed.

Too late, William realized one of the men in the third car was holding another of those damn RPGs on his shoulder. With not enough time to turn, he floored it, hoping the burst of speed would help them outdistance the rocket.

It had almost worked.

27

WILLIAM

The grenade hit the ground just behind them, kicking up an explosion that lifted their rear wheels off the ground.

After that, there was nothing William could do as the tank rolled over onto its hood, screeching along upside-down for another fifty feet or so before finally coming to a halt.

It took him several valuable seconds to regain control of his senses. Claudette was silent beside him, hanging awkwardly from her seatbelt—thank God she'd had it on.

She didn't seem to be injured.

Perhaps she'd fainted?

Or perhaps she…

Panic seizing his throat, he called her name, his voice coming out like a crow's caw. When she didn't respond, he cleared his throat and tried again. "Claudette, are you all right?"

When she groaned, William closed his eyes with relief. He felt like he could breathe again. She was okay. As long as she was alive, everything else could be sorted out.

"We need to get out of here." He struggled to release his seatbelt. Various alarms trilled at him, but he didn't pay them any attention. "Quickly, before they catch up to us." At least one of their pursuers had survived, and William was in no shape for a fight. "We have to—"

Knock. Knock.

A cold thrill of horror went down his spine as he realized it was already too late. A man was there, knocking on his window. William stared at him, took in the bulky man's bloody forehead and sneering grin.

"Open up," the man said in Russian. "Or I'll set your car on fire with you in it."

William didn't doubt that he would. Slowly, he nodded and reached for the control panel that would unlock the door.

"No," Claudette slurred from where she was still hanging. "Don't let him in! He'll kill us!"

She might be right.

Or... William pushed a few buttons, and the doors unlocked. Their would-be killer grinned and jerked the door open—and immediately went into convulsions as millions of volts of electricity flowed into his bare hand.

Thank God Volkov splurged for the deluxe model. Those electrified doors were really something

As William finally managed to release his seatbelt, he fell to the ceiling with an "*oof*" he couldn't quite hold in.

His ribs hadn't been comfortable before, and they were absolutely screaming now. Deactivating the electricity to the doors, he pushed it open and crawled over to the man who'd just promised to burn them alive.

He wasn't moving. He didn't even seem to be breathing.

William felt for his pulse. Nothing. He must have had a heart attack. Now he was doubly glad of the electrified doors. He grabbed the man's gun and checked the magazine—full. Never mind that Lugers weren't his first choice of weapon. Beggars couldn't be choosers.

He crawled back into the car to help Claudette, but she'd already freed herself. Once she got outside she stood up, only tottering a little bit on her heels as she looked around dazedly. "Where…where do we go next?"

William took his jacket off and draped it over her shoulders. She huddled into his leftover warmth gratefully, and he was immediately jealous.

Of his own jacket.

Christ, maybe he had a concussion.

He coughed to clear his throat—and his head. "I checked our position on the GPS right before we crashed," he said. "We're fairly close to the extraction point. It's just under three miles northeast of here."

She blinked and stared at the forest. "I'm going to have to walk…in heels…through that…at night."

"I'll help you," he said. "We'll make it."

"I know we will. I trust you, it's just…." She shivered, then shook her head. "I'm sorry, I just feel exhausted all of a sudden."

Adrenaline crash. She wasn't going to be on her feet for much longer. They needed to get to the extraction point as fast as possible. Sirens wailed in the distance, closing in fast.

They needed to leave all this wreckage behind right the hell now.

"Come on." He tucked her hand into the corner of his arm. "Lean on me." She did, and he led her into the darkness.

William could have used a torch, but he didn't know what kind of response was being mustered against them right now, and he didn't want to risk them being seen if he could help it. The moon was full, the sky was clear, and this part of the forest canopy wasn't so dense that he couldn't pick out a decent path once his eyes adapted to the dark. He guided Claudette over roots and around bushes, wincing in sympathy when random branches reached out and scratched her bare legs.

It was still slow going.

At one point, Claudette started cursing her heels. "I swear to God, I'm bringing flats back in vogue," she muttered after tripping for the umpteenth time in the past mile. "The next fundraiser or red carpet I'm on—flats. Gorgeous, practical flats."

"I'm sure you'll start a trend," William said, keeping his voice deliberately light. He could hear the fatigue beneath her bravado and knew that the real reason she was tripping so much now was that she was too cold, too tired, and on the verge of breaking down.

He put one of her arms around his shoulders, lifting her a little more. "We're close."

"How can you even tell in the dark?"

Honestly? It was a sixth sense by now, an innate knowledge of the spots his handler preferred when it came to extraction points. They were very close and, William thought with a sinking heart, likely too late to make this one.

His fear was confirmed a few minutes later when he caught sight of a small, glowing green dot in the underbrush. It could have been mistaken for an animal's eyes catching the light if there had been two of them.

"We missed the window."

"No," Claudette murmured, pressing her free hand to her face. "Oh no, no. Please, no."

"We'll make the next one," William promised.

He eased her to the ground, then went over and inspected the package. It held the standard equipment: field DPMs for himself and Claudette, thank goodness, as well as prepackaged food and water, a very basic med kit, fresh weapons, fire starters, a GPS transmitter, and a note.

Transmitter coverage is spotty from here on out, so don't rely on it. Meet us at the secondary rendezvous point at 1800 hours in two days' time. Further evacuation after that point isn't guaranteed.

In other words, be there or be square.

"Here." He handed Claudette the new outfit, along with a pair of boots in her size. "These should make the next part easier."

She smiled as she held them up to herself. "Thank you, William. I don't know what I'd do without you."

Oh, you'd probably be perfectly safe, running heists on the side while saving your father's life instead of risking your own life in goddamn Russia.

"No worries," he replied, stiff with the effort of keeping his self-recrimination at bay. "It's my job."

28

CLAUDETTE

"We need to keep going." William put a hand on Claudette's shoulder.

She curled into a ball. "Give me just a few more minutes."

"You've got two. You don't want to be late for the second extraction point, do you?"

She groaned. "No."

After reaching the initial and very discouraging point, they'd continued on foot for two more hours before she'd reached such a level of exhaustion that she couldn't take another step.

At that point, sleep hadn't been just advisable. It had been a necessity.

She'd tried to keep up a stiff upper lip, but the truth was that she'd been on the verge of tears during the entire trek, and not only because she was so bloody tired.

Those past few hours had been the worst of her life—and given that she'd suffered through some that had been quite horrible, that was saying something.

The bungled heist of Clarence House was the most recent and probably the worst and the most detrimental to her future, but it hadn't been as embarrassing as what had happened at her first black-tie event. She'd tripped down the stairs during her introduction, accidentally showing her panties to half the British peerage and breaking her wrist.

Thankfully, William had noticed the state she'd been in, found them a hidden spot to rest, and let her sleep for a couple of hours while he'd kept watch.

Hopefully, those two hours had been enough for her to keep going.

Pushing to her feet, she was tempted to fall back down to the ground in a heap, but one look at the dark circles beneath William's eyes and the gingerly way he held himself helped stiffen her spine and firm her resolve.

He must be even more tired than she was, and he was injured, but he'd watched over her, ignoring his injuries and forcing himself to stay awake and protect her sleeping arse. He had to hurt worse than she did right now, yet she was letting him do all the work of keeping them both safe.

Well, but why not? It was his job, after all.

Don't be petty. It's not attractive. Her mother's voice was far too loud in her head, but that didn't make her wrong. Claudette swallowed her complaints, both at standing and being treated as less able than William himself, and nodded to him. "Shall we?"

"We'd better." He looked up at the sky in assessment. "We've got four hours to go until dawn, and it's getting cloudy. I think we'll have to risk the torches." He handed one to her, along with a bottle of water.

Claudette drained the bottle in one long go, wiping her mouth at the end of her never-ending swallow with a sigh of relief. It was only once she'd finished it off that she wondered—"Oh my God, there's more, isn't there? Tell me I didn't just finish all the water!"

William smiled, his white teeth gleaming even in the low light. "You didn't. There's more in the pack, but we should be a bit chary with it anyhow, just in case." He stood up and pulled the pack on, adjusting the straps and fastening it around his waist so that his hips carried the weight instead of his back. Still, it had to be doing a number on his injured ribs.

"I can take that," Claudette offered.

"It weighs two and a half stone."

There was no way she could carry it. How was he doing that?

"Never mind then." She took the torch he offered her, then fell in behind him and plodded off into the night.

It was certainly easier walking around in these boots than in the stilettos, but her heels were covered in blisters she hadn't remembered until right now, her neck and shoulders ached from the crash, and she felt unbalanced in a way that didn't sit right with her. It was an imbalance that came from a lack of confidence, which under other circumstances would have made Claudette laugh.

She was always confident.

Confidence was a shield, and she wielded it with the best of them.

But if confidence was a shield, then competence was a sword, and right now, Claudette felt downright unarmed.

Plodding about in the middle of the night in enemy territory, which this had to count as, and trying to do it stealthily, she was failing miserably.

She thought of herself as an athlete, but somehow she still managed to trip over every root taking up space on this bloody ground and it was just…it was just intolerable.

Unbearable.

It wasn't because it was so physically taxing but because her nerves were shot.

Claudette couldn't quite get the memory of Volkov's heavy body pressing against her out of her head. She wasn't a professional operative, and the few weeks of training with William hadn't been enough. She was unprepared, and on top of that, she was worried about William and her father.

You're all right.

You can do this.

One foot ahead of the other.

Your father needs you.

William was certainly fulfilling his part of the deal, and Claudette needed to do her part.

Getting used to the silence wasn't hard. The sound of her own breathing was enough to keep her occupied, a rhythm she could rely on and use to help her keep pace. William was moving quickly, but not so fast that she couldn't keep up. Every so often, he glanced at the GPS transmitter in his hand and adjusted their heading, but for the most part, Claudette simply let herself sink into the dull, repetitive motion of the forced march without further complaint.

29

CLAUDETTE

They had gotten into a rhythm, resting for five minutes out of every hour to snack on rock-hard protein bars and drink a bit more of their precious water, but they didn't speak.

What was there to say?

Nothing, absolutely nothing…until…

"Stop."

William's quick-whispered warning broke Claudette out of the haze she'd been wandering in, but it was too abrupt to stop her from almost running into his back.

She was able to halt herself at the last moment. "What's—"

"Quiet!"

A bit nettled, Claudette lowered her volume. "What's wrong?" she whispered.

"There's a road up ahead."

Oh, that was good! They could march along that for a while and make even better time. It was still dark out.

Surely, they'd be able to duck into the woods before any incoming cars spotted them.

"And why aren't we already walking on it?" she asked after a pregnant pause in which William didn't even look at her, just kept his gorgeous, infuriating baby blues scanning the distance.

"Because it's currently occupied with people waiting to kill us."

Shite, shite, shite! Bloody hell—

William hunkered down, taking off the pack as he pulled his handgun from where he'd holstered it. He grabbed another gun, small but not as small as the Pico, and handed it to Claudette.

"Stay here," he said, and then—

"No!" She was barely able to keep herself from grabbing his shoulder and hauling him back to her. He couldn't leave her here! How was she supposed to get along without him?

Do you prefer to help him take out a bunch of people who are trying to kill you?

But even before she could answer her own question, William disappeared into the night.

Further self-recrimination was rendered moot as within seconds gunshots sounded, eradicating the stillness of the early morning.

Claudette was frozen on the spot, hoping and praying with every new crack that rent the air that William wasn't hurt. She was sick with guilt, with the remnants of her temper, with the fatigue that still dogged her footsteps and shadowed her every move. She was useless, and if he got hurt because of it…

Bam! Bam! Bam!

The last round echoed with finality, and Claudette blinked her glazed-over eyes and stared desperately at the last place she'd seen William, wishing him to reappear, to make her fears vanish, to let her know that it was all right, that he was okay…

As a hand touched her arm from the side, Claudette screamed and nearly fell, only to find herself pulled into William's firm embrace. "Oh God," she moaned, throwing her arms around his neck and closing her eyes. It took everything she had not to break down in tears right there. "That was awful. Oh my god, don't do that to me again."

William chuckled. "Which part? The leaving you alone or the saving your life?"

"The first one! Obviously saving my life is good, but not when it comes at the expense of yours!"

"Hmm, that's not how this works, but don't worry. I'm barely scratched this time around."

Claudette pulled back and stared at him. "What on earth does that mean? What constitutes a scratch?" She began running her hands over his body, searching for a wound despite his assurances that he was okay.

"I'm fine, really. We should just keep going."

She finally found it on his thigh. "Bloody hell!" she hissed as she found the tear in his trousers. "What, did one of those bastards have a knife?"

"No. A bullet grazed me, but it's—"

"If you tell me it's fine, I will shoot you myself," she snapped, then turned to the backpack. "I'm getting the medical supplies. You, sit down."

He sat with surprising grace. The expression on his face was somewhere between a bit annoyed and...Claudette couldn't name the other, much softer emotion she saw there. Or perhaps she was just afraid to. Either way, he stayed obediently still while she cleaned the wound and used all of the gauze in the kit to staunch it before bandaging it as best she could.

"MI-bloody-6 and you can't even splurge on a decent med kit," she muttered as she finished up. "You're going to bleed through that in minutes."

"It'll be all right," William said as he got to his feet and shouldered the backpack. "Once we're extracted, I'll have one of the medics look at it."

"Oh, so in thirty-six hours or so."

"Yeah. That's about right." William's mask dropped for a moment, and his fatigue showed through.

Claudette felt like slapping herself.

He just shot people—killed to keep me safe. And I repay him by picking a fight with him.

Not that she was wrong, but now wasn't the time to harp on it. She sighed and straightened up. "Lead on. And...thank you."

William smiled at her, soft and warm, then turned and headed out again at an angle to where they'd been walking before. Was he diverting around the bodies so she wouldn't have to see them?

Very gentlemanly of him.

30

CLAUDETTE

They didn't have any more scares for the rest of the morning, and by noon, the forest had given way to an open expanse of a field dotted with a few small houses here and there.

William's smile was long gone, and he scowled at the landscape like it had just insulted his mother. "I don't like it," he said.

"Do we have a choice?" Claudette asked.

"Unfortunately, we don't. Going around will take us into even less friendly territory."

She shrugged. "Then it's 'keep calm and carry on,' I suppose."

"I suppose." William looked at her with a serious expression on his face. "We need to do this fast. Run for the first house and assess the situation once we get there." He gave her a stern look. "Don't stop no matter what happens. Just keep running. I'll be right behind you."

He wanted her to go first?

She swallowed. "Got it."

"All right." He looked out over the seemingly empty field, gun in firing position. "Go. Now."

Claudette emerged from the trees and broke into a run. Her legs didn't want to cooperate, and her lungs were pitching a fit, but the rush that came from suddenly being out in the sun after so much time in the dark carried her forward. She made it to the side of the first house without issue, and a second later, William joined her there.

She glanced down at his leg and winced. The blood had soaked the fabric over his entire thigh. At this rate, he was going to give them away by leaking all over the place.

"This is ridiculous," she hissed as emphatically and quietly as she could. "You can't keep this up. You need a fresh bandage and preferably some stitches to keep it all together instead of bleeding like a stuck pig."

William grimaced. "Well, we don't have anything, so—"

"Wait here." Claudette turned and looked out the window at the back of the house. No movement. There was no vehicle to be seen. She darted around to the front porch before William could do more than grab at her arm and miss.

Ha.

Time to earn my keep.

Breaking in through the front door was child's play. There were no cameras, only one lock, and a brief inspection of the downstairs revealed it to be not only devoid of people but also free of pets.

Perfect.

Claudette paused her inspection to wave to William through the window.

He did not seem to appreciate the gesture.

Five minutes of searching later, she emerged from the house with a medical kit in her hands.

He glared at her. "What the hell do you think you're—"

"Are we going to waste time arguing, or are we going to find a safe spot to hunker down for long enough to get your leg seen to?"

He ground his teeth but nodded, pointing to their next destination.

The run-and-hide, hopscotch approach to getting to the forest on the other side of the break in their route took half an hour, but at least the fight was well and truly out of William by the time they were done with it.

Once they were safely in the shadow again, Claudette motioned for him to sit down.

He didn't argue, just set the pack up against a tree and then used it as a backrest as he sat down.

Poor thing.

Claudette ripped the hole in his trousers a little wider, frowning as the blood stained her hands, then opened up the very well-stocked medical kit she'd found in the house.

William barely hissed as she cleaned and dried the wound. By the time she'd finished and had used her backup safety pin, his face was gray with fatigue.

When he tried to get up, she held on to his hand, keeping him beside her. "You need a break," she insisted.

"So do you, but we must keep going," he replied.

Claudette frowned. "How far is the extraction point now?"

William looked at the GPS unit, even though he had their position memorized. "We've got another fifteen miles to go."

"And we have until tomorrow evening to get there, right?"

"Tomorrow at six p.m., that's not exactly late enough to—"

"It's late enough," Claudette insisted. "We can afford a little break, can't we?"

William was doing his best to keep his expression fixed, but she could see the cracks around the edges of it now. She decided to push her luck.

"We'll be better off for it," she said, very reasonably, she thought. "A chance to rest and recuperate a little. No more than a few hours, and I know I'll be feeling fit again."

"You're already fit."

Oh, was that a compliment slipping through?

Claudette grinned even though she knew that, more than anything else, it was a sure sign that William was tired. Apart from a few moments of tenderness during training, he'd done his best not to let any of his softer feelings through. Now more than ever though, Claudette knew he had feelings for her. As he kept pointing out, saving her life was his job, but being considerate of her feelings? Complimenting her? That was a choice, something he did just because he wanted to.

From the look on his face, he knew he'd slipped up too. Rather than getting into an argument about what was or wasn't appropriate behavior between the two of them, Claudette averted her eyes and stuffed the rest of the new supplies into the old med kit. "Maybe not here, though," she said. "We're still pretty close to the field, and we don't want to make it easy for someone to catch a glimpse of us if we can help it. Right? That's operational security."

"Something like that," William agreed. He took the water bottle Claudette passed him and drained it, then reached for the pack.

"Nope." She jerked it out of his reach and slung it onto her back before he could further protest.

"Claudette…"

"I've got it," she assured him even though she wasn't sure she could carry the pack for any length of time. "You have your gun on you, and this thing has dropped a half-stone since we've been snacking so much. I can carry it for a while."

William sighed. "Fine. But only for a little bit."

She nodded. "Of course."

She wasn't trying to take the reins, she just wanted him to know that she was grateful for what he was doing for her and that she realized how he felt about her, even if he wasn't ready to confess.

Claudette saw it, and she felt it right back.

31

WILLIAM

The pack was too heavy for Claudette, but she didn't let it show, keeping a brisk pace.

William was so proud of her.

Letting her take the lead was, at the same time, one of the easiest and one of the least comfortable things he'd ever done. He trusted her and knew he could rely on her, yet it didn't sit well with him that he'd let her shoulder the load.

He was supposed to be taking care of her, not the other way around. She was his responsibility, damn it. Had he done such a shitty job looking after her that she didn't even believe he could keep carrying the damn pack?

Not that she was wrong.

In the last twelve hours he got her into a car crash, got her shot at, and potentially burned alive, so that was maybe not a road he wanted to go down.

William was perceptive enough to know that he was projecting right now and that it was more about him than her. Claudette seemed genuinely happy to have the chance to take on some more responsibility—not to mention weight—and give him a chance to rest his leg.

He didn't want to acknowledge it, but the way the area was heating up, it was very likely that an infection was setting in. He'd taken the general-spectrum antibiotic the med kit had offered, but not being able to let the leg rest was taking its toll. A break would be good. Something they could afford.

After all, they had over twenty-four hours to reach the extraction point.

She needed it. And, if he was honest with himself, he needed it even more.

He let her take the lead, changing her course as needed with a few words or a light tap on her shoulder.

After walking for another hour and a half, they were back in the deep forest, and as the sounds of civilization had faded away into a distant buzz, William finally called a stop, but only because he could see Claudette was beginning to flag.

"We can stop here."

"Really?" She swiped a strand of hair back from her face as she looked around the little clearing he'd indicated. It was nothing but fallen leaves and bumpy roots, with little but the remoteness to recommend it. "Are you sure? I can keep going. I'm up for it."

"I know you are." Did he ever know that.

William was being shamed at his own game by this woman, and part of him loved it. "But I'm about to drop, and this place is as good as any for us to take a little time to recover."

"If you say so." She set down the pack with an audible sigh of relief, then gestured toward the trees. "I'm just going to go and…you know."

William hid his smile. "I know. Go ahead. I'll be here."

As she wandered a bit deeper into the forest, he arranged the pack in such a way that they could both lean against it and got down onto the ground.

Staring up at the sunlight filtering through the canopy, William wondered what the hell he was going to do.

You can't fall in love with her.

It was already too late. The best thing he could do for himself at this point, for both of them, was to keep her from getting in too deep. It was one thing for him to be a fool, quite another for him to let her love him back.

How was he going to pull that off?

William couldn't remember the last time he'd been in love, the last time his whole body had felt more alive just being around someone. Claudette drew him in like she was his magnetic north.

He wanted to always be looking at her, listening to her, holding her…

Doing more with her.

Thank God he was too tired to get hard right now, because that was the last thing he needed to deal with on top of the rest of this clusterfuck.

Maybe it's not really love. You've barely seen another woman for weeks. You're wrapped up in each other, totally and completely. It's easy to get carried away when things are so intense.

Only William knew the difference by now. He'd been

infatuated with a few of his female instructors before, and with some of the agents he'd worked with before Liam had decided he was better in solo operations. He knew what it felt like to be drawn in by competence or proximity, and this was different.

Even now, when Claudette was filthy from the hike and exhausted beyond all measure, and as far as she could be from the fleet-footed thief or belle of the ball that he'd seen in action before, William couldn't stop thinking about her.

Wanting to touch her, wanting to be with her, wanting... Wanting.

Too much wanting for him to face.

Too much wanting for his heart to bear.

"Whew!" Claudette collapsed next to him with a groan.

William did his best not to react beyond opening his eyes to look her way. He wanted to pull her into his arms, cradle her against his chest, capture her mouth in a kiss as his hands moved lower until...

"You okay?" he asked politely.

"Good question," Claudette replied, reaching down to unlace her boots.

She removed one off and pulled her sock down, inspecting the sizable bandages she'd put over the blisters she'd developed. "Objectively? I'm alive and able to walk, so I'm quite well. Subjectively, I don't mind telling you that if I never see another boot again, it will be too soon."

"You've got it in for the shoe industry," he teased her, which—God, he should have just let it drop, not engaged in fucking banter. What the fuck was wrong with him? Too late to stop now, though. "First the heels, now the boots."

"I did say I'm a flats girl from here on out, right?" she said, then nudged him with her shoulder. "Come on. You can't tell me there isn't some article of clothing out there that you loathe beyond all reason. Everybody hates something, even if it's just a death match of briefs versus boxers."

William shrugged. "I wear whatever the job requires. I'm as at home in a tuxedo as I am in a Speedo."

Shut up, William!

Claudette, though, laughed with delight. "Have you worn many Speedos over the course of your spy career?"

Was he blushing? He hoped not. "Sometimes, I have to work in a tropical location. Occasionally, that means a Speedo."

"Yes, but do you like them?" Claudette pressed. "I mean, thongs make my arse look bloody fantastic, but that doesn't mean I like flossing my lady parts with lace for hours at a time."

"Oh my God," William groaned.

She laughed again, probably thinking he was embarrassed.

Nope, he was just trying to keep the image of Claudette walking around in a thong from the front of his brain. His hold over his self-control was tenuous at best right now. If he wanted to distract her, the easiest thing to do would be to talk about himself.

"Crocs," he said at last. "I don't like them. I did a job on a yacht once, and after one of the windows was blown out, there was glass everywhere. A piece of it went straight through the bottom of the shoe into my foot. I had to hobble away from that job. So there, I don't like Crocs."

"Mm. That's fair." Perhaps unconsciously, Claudette leaned her head against his shoulder. "What else don't you like?"

"Hmm…fedoras. They're so pretentious, I can't bloody stand them. And trucker hats. God save us from American fashion. If I never have to wear another trucker hat, it will be too soon."

Her laugh was more of a breath than anything else. She was falling asleep. "What else?" she whispered.

"I don't like braces," he said after a moment. "They feel one wrong turn away from snapping every second I'm in them. I don't care for ascots, although they make a great gag in a pinch." He winced; was that too much? But Claudette didn't say anything. "I'm not in love with herringbone tweed," he murmured, hearing her breathing settle. "Makes me feel old when I wear it. And latex anything leaves me feeling slimy, like I'm trying to lure girls into a van or something like that."

"I like silk. Cashmere. Egyptian cotton. I like things that are soft but hard all at once. Things that endure. Things that are built to last." He turned to look down at Claudette, who had fallen fast asleep. "I like you," he told her, the honesty in his voice so raw he was grateful she couldn't hear him. "I like you so much."

32

CLAUDETTE

His hand touches my face, trailing down the side of my neck and lightly brushing over my collarbone. I gasp as it goes even lower, fingers warm against my breast as he rubs his thumb over my nipple. It's so much already, so much more than I ever knew was possible with him, and so delicious I know I want more. I take his hand and lower it down, along my stomach, and past my hip until finally, he's right there at my entrance.

Touch me. Come inside of me, feel me, make me—

"Claudette?"

She snapped back to wakefulness, as shocked as if she'd just had a bucket of ice water thrown over her. She stared up at William, confused as to why he was so far away, and why he was wearing clothes, hadn't he just been…

The throb between her legs—her clothed legs—was enough to ground Claudette back in the real world.

Oh. Oh, damn.

"William?" Her throat was dry.

She felt around for a bottle of water, then accepted the one he held out to her with a sigh. It was cool and refreshing and wiped the rest of the cobwebs out of her brain.

A sex dream. A few hours of sleep had apparently been long enough for her to have a bloody sex dream. Worst of all, she hadn't quite gotten to the part where she got off before being woken up.

She'd better roll with it—there was no time for complaints now. "How long did we sleep?" she asked, pushing onto her knees.

She expected William to offer her a hand up, but instead he reached for the water bottle, capping it and putting it away.

Ooookay then.

Claudette stood up and waited for him to reply. It took longer than it should have, especially given that he couldn't seem to stop looking at her.

"About three hours," he said at last. "Time to get a move on."

"Right." Claudette stretched her arms above her head, getting a delicious series of pops out of her back and shoulders as she did so.

Cripes. Sleeping on the ground: going straight on the list of things she didn't intend to do anymore after this, along with wearing heels.

"Mmmph," she groaned, then bent over to touch her toes.

"Hurry up already," he barked.

Claudette straightened, startled as she looked at William. What had she done to merit that tone from him?

"If we're running late," she began tentatively, "you could have woken me up sooner."

"You needed the rest," he said in a gentler tone than the one he'd just used. It was still far from the warmth she was accustomed to from him, though. "And so did I," he added. "But we've got a long march ahead of us, and there's no time to waste. Do you need to relieve yourself?"

Why is he treating me like a child?

Claudette could figure out whether she needed to dig a hole in the woods for herself, thank you very much.

"I'm fine," she said stiffly. "Let's just go." She reached for the pack, but William picked it up and set it on his back before she could take it. "I can take it," she insisted.

"It's my turn," he said stubbornly. "Lace your boots up, and let's go."

"Fine." She turned away from him to do up her shoes, fighting with a sudden and infuriating influx of tears in her eyes.

Why was he being like this? The entire time they'd been together, he'd never been anything other than perfectly polite. Most of the time, he'd been warm, friendly...even more. But right now, he was treating her as though she was nothing but a burden.

There was no conversation as they restarted their march. William led the way, and Claudette followed him, practically boring holes into the back of his head with her eyes as she stared at him, wondering.

Was it because he was hurt?

Injuries could make anyone short-tempered, and the one on his leg was just the most obvious wound. He'd been favoring his ribs earlier, so perhaps that was getting worse. Perhaps he was being so brusque because he needed to get them to the extraction point before he couldn't move at all.

Except, William didn't seem to be any worse off now than he had been before. If anything, the rest really had done him some good. His gait seemed smoother, steps long and even. So if it wasn't because he was in more pain, then what was the reason for his coldness?

What had she done, or said, or—

Oh. Oh no. Her dream, her wet dream, the one where he'd been about to—surely she hadn't—

Had she called out to him? Said his name, moved against him, touched him in some way he didn't want to be touched?

She was swamped with feelings of guilt and shame, so heavy they almost stopped her in her tracks.

Good God, what kind of a person was she? How could she, even in her sleep, be thinking about getting off when they were literally on the run for their lives in the middle of fucking nowhere? No wonder he was pissed—she probably would be, too, if the person she was sworn to protect had decided to turn the whole blasted affair into some kind of kinky fantasy.

The mere thought of it was enough to put a damper on Claudette's ire, as well as her energy. The hike became a trudge, the reality of what she'd done an iron bar across her back that made it hard to keep pace with the man she'd seemingly offended. Rather than stare at him, she kept her eyes firmly on the ground.

Just a few more miles, and then he'll be rid of you, and you of him.

It couldn't come soon enough.

33

CLAUDETTE

The first break after the nap was a tense one. Claudette refused to look directly at William, and in turn, he was nearly silent as he split a protein bar between them. It put her on edge, something she loathed, especially when she was with someone she liked.

By the second break, her behavior was apparently off enough that even William wondered about it.

"Claudette? Are you all right?" he asked when the silence seemed to be too much.

"Fine," she said dully, taking the water he handed to her without making eye contact.

"Are you sure? Do you need a painkiller, or would you like a longer break—"

"I said I'm fucking fine!" she snapped, then instantly blushed. Argh, fucking, why had she brought up fucking? He was going to think she was referring to the dream!

But William didn't seem to make that connection. He just looked at her with a vague air of hurt, as though she were the one who was being strange and unreliable when it was clearly him.

She huffed and turned away from him, and after a minute, he set the pack down and walked off into the trees with a quiet, "Back in a moment."

By the time night rolled around, Claudette had been walking for almost twenty-four hours, and she was feeling every damn step. Her blisters burned, her neck hurt, and her heart downright ached. And with every passing hour, her shame became increasingly subsumed by a sense of righteous indignation.

After all, it's not like you can help what you do while asleep.

Even if she had said his name, which Claudette wasn't sure she had, she'd been bloody sleeping! He couldn't seriously take offense at something she did while asleep. Perhaps she'd made him uncomfortable, but then he'd turned around and repaid the favor by making her feel downright disliked when she woke up, and now he had the gall to act as though he was saddened by her distance?

Wasn't that what he wanted?

Or did he only want it when he was the one who was distancing himself?

By the time William called a halt at midnight, Claudette had had it. "What's your problem?" she demanded, putting her hands on her hips and glaring at him.

"What?" William seemed confused at first, then defensive. "What are you talking about?"

"I'm talking about your ruddy problem with me! I don't know what it is or why you're acting so strange, but I'd like to clear it up now if you don't mind. Tell me what I did to make you act like such a sodding bastard to me."

"I haven't been—"

"Yes, you have!" she interrupted before he could try to tell her she'd been imagining it. "From the moment I woke up, you've been distant and weird with me. I don't know why—" at least she hoped she didn't know why "—but whatever's going on, you need to talk to me about it. Aren't we adults? Aren't we friends?" Her voice broke a little on the last word, but she kept going. "Can't we go back to that? Please?"

William looked pained. "I'm sorry," he said quietly. "It's not that I don't want to be friends. I just—you see, I'm—"

"What?" Claudette asked, closing the distance between them until they were nearly touching. "You're what? Just tell me!"

William froze.

At first, Claudette thought he was freezing because he still didn't know what to say or how to say it, that he was still trying to string her along and convince her this was her fault when he was the one who'd changed, but then he suddenly reached out and crushed her to his chest with one hand while pulling his gun with the other.

Now it was her turn to freeze. She didn't know what he'd heard or sensed, she certainly hadn't sensed it herself, but she trusted him.

I still trust him. No matter what else has changed, I trust him...wait...is he...

"They've got dogs," he whispered, seemingly unaware of

exactly what Claudette was pressed against. "You need to get up the tree behind me."

Claudette looked at it nervously, clutching William tight. "I don't think I can reach the bottom branch," she replied.

"I'll give you a leg-up." He backed them quietly toward the tree, then put just enough space between them so that he could position his thigh like a step. "One, two, three."

Claudette was up and into the tree before three was even done. She pulled herself onto the lowest branch, then up a few more. It didn't feel like much of a hiding place. Even with the leaves, it seemed exposed, and of course, the dogs would be able to smell where they'd just been. Maybe William had some sort of trick for that?

"William?" she called out softly.

Nothing.

"William?" she tried it a little louder, just a tiny bit. Still no reply.

The urge to go back down and check on him ran up against the absolute stupidity of that plan. He'd told her to get up here, helped her get up—she needed to damn well stay up here until he told her it was safe to come back down. Surely, he'd join her in a moment. She just needed to be patient.

Only he didn't join her. One minute passed, two, and he didn't come up after her. Stupid or not, Claudette was a few seconds away from jumping back down and finding him when she heard the low growl of a dog.

Oh, God.

She clung to the branch, hiding her face against the bark. She wasn't typically afraid of dogs, not even when working a job, but these weren't someone's prized pet or aggressive yard dogs. That was probably a highly trained attack animal, and William was down there all by himself, and yes, she trusted him, but how could he possibly defend himself against a pack of—

She heard a faint hiss and a thud, followed by a round of barks so pathetic she could hardly believe they came from the same animal that had been growling a moment ago. The barks turned to whines, and the whines became fainter and fainter. After a minute, she could barely hear the dog at all. After two, it was gone entirely.

What the hell just happened?

"Claudette?"

"William!" She detached herself from the branch and swung down, awkwardly landing on the ground.

He was there immediately though, picking her up and making sure she was all right.

"What happened?" There was the faintest scent of... "Did you use pepper spray on it?"

"I did." He pointed back the way they'd come. "The handler sent it out on its own to track us down. That was a mistake, but it had a radio collar broadcasting its position. We need to move before they find us again."

Claudette rubbed her arms. "How close are we to the extraction point?" she asked.

"It's seven miles away."

Seven miles. That wasn't so bad. She could do that in a couple of hours, and then they could settle in and talk about—

"But we're going to have to do some more evasion techniques on the way there, or I don't think we'll make it," William continued. Her brief elation vanished. "At the very least, we've got to cross a few rivers."

Oh, Lord, no. "There are rivers?"

"More like streams," he assured her. "Just to muddle our scents. I used the rest of the pepper spray about a hundred feet back that way, so any dogs coming from that direction will be warned off. Hopefully, that will buy us the time we need."

"William."

He looked at her, honest and forthright, the way she was used to. "What is it?"

Can you tell me why you had a massive erection when you pulled me against you a few minutes ago? Were you thinking of me?

Do you want me?

Now wasn't the time for those thoughts. "Is there any more pepper spray?" she asked resignedly.

"No. We have a few smoke grenades, but no more pepper spray." He squeezed her shoulder, and she leaned into the touch. "It's all right. Just listen to me, keep your weapon ready, and we'll be fine. We're going to get through this, I promise."

"I know we will." For the first time in hours, since he'd ripped her heart to pieces by putting distance between them for reasons Claudette thought she might understand a little better now, she trusted that they were going to get through this.

They, friends and colleagues, and maybe more, were going to get through this.

34

WILLIAM

The second part of their journey to the extraction point was everything William had been hoping to avoid with this escape.

They'd been found—not completely, but clearly their general location was known to the people they were trying to hide from. That meant that despite the cover of trees and the darkness, they had to take extra steps to avoid being discovered—doubling back, laying down false trails, fording rivers, and above all, avoiding roads and houses and any place someone might be waiting to catch a glimpse of them.

There were no more naps. William barely stopped for breaks. They were being hunted, and it was his job to make sure that he denied the Russians their prey.

No one was going to be taking Claudette anywhere except for him.

He could see that it was hard on her, but at least the tension between them—the tension that he'd put there, fool that he was—was gone now.

She'd let him help her over logs, let him tie the two of them together as they'd waded across a hip-deep stretch of water that had left her shivering with cold. She'd clung to him for assistance and comfort, and he'd welcomed her in every time.

I love you.

He couldn't deny it.

He wouldn't let himself deny it, not when doing so caused her pain. If the worst came to the worst and he was killed, he wouldn't have her last memory of him be aloofness on his part. Besides, she'd clearly noticed the hard-on he'd gotten during their confrontation right before the dog found them.

The "I'm above this" ship had sailed.

He couldn't help it. She was perfect. Even when she was arguing with him and driving him nuts, she was perfect. He'd never met a woman who appealed to him in so many ways before. It was enough to make him want to envision a future for them, as impossible as that seemed.

But the future, whatever it was, could wait. Right now, he had to make sure she survived this bloody mission.

"We're getting close," he promised her as they made their way through yet another section of forest, this one with more pine trees.

The needles crunched softly beneath their feet, giving walking almost a springy feel, which was good. His feet ached obscenely at this point, which meant hers had to feel positively murderous. "These extraction points are well-chosen. I promise there'll be a safe place for us to rest and wait to get picked up."

"That's good," she said, sounding a bit listless. "Rest will be good."

"It will. I know I'm pushing you hard, and I'm sorry for that, but I also know that you're going to make it." For some reason, he wasn't able to shut his mouth—maybe he was getting a bit delirious with fatigue as well? But it didn't matter. Every word seemed to draw her up a little straighter. "You're tough. One of the toughest people I've ever met. I'm amazed at how strong you are. You're one of a kind in every way, and I'm going to make sure you get to your father in time. Got it?"

"Got it," she said, chuckling a little. "Thanks for the pep talk, coach."

"You're welcome, sport," he replied, and she laughed again.

Pleased that Claudette was moving better, William turned his attention to the landscape in front of them. They were headed toward a private airport, once belonging to another Russian warmonger who'd insisted on building hangars, warehouses, a landing strip, and a helicopter pad to keep his dirty business running. He'd been removed from that business and from breathing a decade ago now, but his property had yet to be repurposed. It was the perfect spot for an extraction.

Which, of course, meant that it was one of the places their pursuers would probably be monitoring. William was sure his handler had thought of ways around that, but in order for those ways to benefit them, they had to make it onto airport grounds and find the secure location Liam had prepared for them.

35

WILLIAM

"Oh, come on," Claudette groaned as she saw the chain-link fence looming before them.

They were fortunate it was a foggy morning instead of sunny like yesterday. It would give them a bit more cover, but speed was still going to be of the essence.

"Tell me we don't have to climb that."

"I could tell you that, but I'd be lying," William said.

"Why can't we cut through it? You've got wire clippers in that sack of yours. I saw them."

"We don't want to leave behind any evidence that we were here," William replied. Luckily, the ground was firm, instead of the muddy mess they'd slogged through in other spots. "Trust me, the easiest thing to do is climb. Besides," he added more lightly, "I happen to know you're excellent at getting into places you shouldn't."

"I am," Claudette replied archly, then sighed. "At least when I've got plenty of sleep and three cups of espresso in me."

Fresh guilt surged through him. "This is the last big hurdle," he assured her. "Once we're inside, we'll be way more secure. It'll just be a matter of settling in and waiting for pickup." He looked up at the top of the fence and grimaced. Barbed wire. He'd be losing this coat, then.

"What makes you think they won't look for us here?"

"I'm not sure that they won't, but there are many other spots on this trajectory that will look even more appealing to them." He took off first the pack and then his jacket. "After all, we're effectively caging ourselves in by using this location." *Aaand* it was time to stop talking about it because Claudette's eyes were getting wider and wider. He didn't want to scare her. "Okay, I'm going to go up first and throw my jacket over the wiring at the top. Watch how I use it for protection as I crawl over, then copy that."

"You know, this wasn't part of the training," she said conversationally as she watched him redo the pack. "I feel like that was a bit of an oversight under the circumstances. Consider this a formal complaint—more barbed wire during preparations, please."

William grinned. "I'll make sure to pass that along." Then he turned to the fence and shook out his hands.

All right. Time to get this done.

Climbing the fence was not easy, but not impossible. His leg burned, his feet ached, and his ribs had seen better times, but William had trained for years to ignore his body's complaints. He got to the top, carefully secured his thick camouflage jacket over a section of barbed wire, then eased himself over it. The coil was about two feet wide—not so bad for him, but it would be harder for Claudette since he had eight inches in height on her.

She'd handle it. Or he'd go back up and carry her over himself.

Finally, he touched down on the broken asphalt on the other side.

Claudette gave him a very quiet round of applause, which he bowed for, then began the climb herself. The first part was easy enough, but once she got to the top—

"Ow, shite," she hissed as she threw her leg over.

"Are you all right?"

"If you call being pricked by this bloody thing two inches away from my cunny all right, then I suppose I am," she ground out. "Damn it, that bloody hurts."

"Do you need me to come and help you?" Because he would, in a heartbeat.

"No, I've got it. I—hang on." She made it over, then paused long enough to wrangle his jacket off and toss it down to him. William had been planning to go back up and get it himself, but he appreciated Claudette taking care of it.

She finally got to the ground, setting her feet down with a wince. "Right, let's not do that again if we can help it."

"Your wish is my command," William assured her. "Stick close to me from here on out. We've still got to be careful."

Claudette nodded, and William turned and quick-marched them across what was probably once a parking lot, until they reached the nearest hangar. He glanced inside the dirty window—empty. Not for them, then.

The next two buildings, a shed, and a small warehouse, were also empty. The fourth, though, appeared to be full of shelving. Some of it was empty, some of it was covered in ancient, dusty tarps, and some of it was so far back in the darkness that he couldn't see whether or not it was occupied. It would give them decent cover, though.

Judging from the six faint scratch marks on the windowsill, whoever had set this extraction point up felt the same. "Here's our stop," he said, reaching for the decrepit-looking window. It rose smoothly, without even a squeak from the swollen or rotting wood.

He helped Claudette in, then entered the warehouse himself. The entire place smelled stale, but he could just make out a section of flooring that was slightly less dusty than the others. He led the way until he got to a filthy piece of tarp on a broad, mid-level shelf. He pulled it back and—

"Ah."

"Wow." Claudette looked over his shoulder with wide eyes. "That's pretty nice, all things considered."

It was. Behind the tarp was a cozy space with two clean sleeping bags, fresh bottles of water, a small electric lantern, and another cache of protein bars. There was room for their pack, too. William stepped aside and motioned to their new home for the next ten hours. "Ladies first."

"A gentleman under every circumstance," Claudette teased him as she crawled inside. She began pulling out one of the sleeping bags while William concerned himself with covering their tracks.

36

WILLIAM

It took some time before they were settled. Having the space for two sleeping bags was nice, but it was still, well, just a couple of body bags spread out next to each other when you got right down to it. Once they figured it out, though, and found that they could both sit up straight without their heads touching the shelf above them, Claudette settled into a downright cheerful mood.

"Plug your lovely nose," she warned William with a smirk as she tugged on her right boot. "Because this is coming off whether you like it or not."

"Do you want help treating your heels?" he asked, diplomatically sidestepping the chance to complain, however jokingly. "Those blisters must be killing you."

"Honestly, it's the jab along my thigh that's really getting to me. Good thing I've had my tetanus booster, because—"

"Damn, right." How could he have forgotten that she got injured climbing into this place? "Take your trousers off. Let me get a look at it."

"Agent Kentworth!" Claudette pressed a hand to her chest in mock scandal. "How very forward of you, sir! I'll have you know that I'm a lady, and I don't take my trousers off for just anyone."

William grinned at her. "But you'll take them off for me, right? I've got Germolene." He waved the small tube of antiseptic cream at her.

"Ooh, you do know how to sweet-talk a girl. Fine. But be gentle." Claudette got her other boot and the camouflage trousers off. William had to hide a wince at just how many bruises she was sporting—he'd had no idea.

Yet her legs are still the most gorgeous thing ever.

Claudette tapped her inner thigh. "My wound is up here," she said, still playful. William ignored the blush he knew had to be rising in his cheeks and inspected the puncture she'd gotten coming over the barbed wire.

It wasn't deep at all. More uncomfortable had to be the scratches on either side of it. He applied the ointment with careful fingers, then covered the worst section with a bandage. "There," he said, looking her in the eyes. "All better."

"Thank you." They stared at each other for a long, tense moment. William felt the urge to move, to act, to draw closer to her and cup the nape of her neck in his hand and bring her sweet lips into a kiss. He almost moved to do so, except Claudette suddenly shivered. Not the sexy kind of shiver, either. The warehouse was cooler than it had been outside, and even with the sleeping bags, the racks they were on were a hard metal that shared their chill readily.

"You must be exhausted," William said, berating himself

internally. Of course, she bloody was. She needed rest—they had plenty of time before extraction. Sleep was the best thing for her. He would keep watch. "Lie down, take a nap. Unless you're hungry?"

She smiled a bit wanly. "I think it'll be a while before I'm ready for another protein bar, but thank you. Maybe—" She yawned, only belatedly raising a hand to cover her mouth. "Ugh, sorry. Maybe you're right."

"I'm always right."

"Don't get ahead of yourself," Claudette cautioned with a smile as she lay down in the bag and pulled it up to her chin. Completely unselfconscious, she shut her eyes and snuggled in. "Don't be 'fraid to wake me up, yeah?" she mumbled as exhaustion took over more of her faculties. "I'll be...r'dy to go inna sec, no worries."

"I'm not worried." For once, William wasn't. They had shelter, they had decent security, and they had the promise of escape. "Go to sleep."

"Mmm..." She drifted off between one breath and the next, going lax as she slipped into slumber. William watched her for a long moment, then slid down from their shelter-shelf and crossed over to the window they came in through. He looked carefully outside, scanning the sky for drones, listening cautiously for the sound of dogs or men, or even vehicles.

Nothing. They were utterly alone.

Good. He could risk a message with the transmitter, then. He tapped it in, hoping Liam got it soon. *At B. Clear for now. On schedule?*

He got a written reply back in seconds. *Yes. Sit tight.*

Exercising the dogs. William grinned. That was code for the series of backups MI6 had prepared to keep them safe being put to effective use. *All is well?*

Liam didn't usually bother to ask when they were working with third parties. He must have a bit of a soft spot for Claudette after all. William typed back *Yes*, then after another minute with no reply turned the transmitter off.

That was it. His last real duty, seen to. Not that he was off the hook from here on out—of course not. But their backup was finally in play, and they were in the safest spot they could be, and soon enough, they'd be on a plane, or a helicopter, or in a secure vehicle making their way back to England. And then…

Don't think about it. Don't think about losing her.

Besides, how could he lose what he'd never really had in the first place?

William wasn't going to sleep himself, but there wasn't much for him to do now. He meditated for a bit, put a few booby traps up to keep intruders from getting very far, then sat down on his sleeping bag and just…stared at Claudette. She was beautiful, always beautiful to him, whether she was well-rested or exhausted.

William lay beside her and cataloged every inch of her face: the lay of her eyelashes against her cheeks, the sweet curve of her nose, the soft angles of her cheek and jaw that he wanted to kiss again and again. He took in everything, all that he could, and then closed his eyes and committed it to memory. For the rest of his life, he'd be able to bring this moment back to mind whenever he wanted—a trick he'd learned in training. However, this was much better than memorizing a numeric code or a blueprint. This was his beloved, the first person he'd ever put above a mission. He already knew that he'd put her first every time if he had to. It was probably for the best she didn't know that, because…because…

Because she was awake. Because she was looking right back at him with stars in her eyes, and this time, she reached out first. "William," Claudette whispered as she touched his cheek. "Please tell me it's not just me."

"It's not just you," he managed at last. "It's not. You're… you don't even know what you do to me. What I want to do to you."

Claudette smiled and eased herself a bit closer. "Why don't you show me what you have in mind?" she asked, her seductive energy back at full power. William stared at her for a long moment, gauging her sincerity and wondering when exactly he'd reached the point of no return.

It didn't matter. She wanted him now, and oh, how he wanted her. He turned his face to kiss her palm, then slid his arms around her waist and pulled her in close to him, finally capturing her mouth in a kiss.

William felt like he was flying. It was everything he'd dreamed of already. And there was the promise of so much more to come.

37

CLAUDETTE

Claudette was drowning.
Drowning in heat. In desire.

She couldn't remember the last time she'd been so incredibly turned on so quickly. It was so different from her usual exploits—so much better in every way.

This wasn't some posh chap she'd met at a club or been forced to socialize with at a society "to-do."

This was William—a man unlike any other she'd met before.

It wasn't just his rugged masculinity or gorgeous face and piercing blue eyes. She'd met many handsome men who did nothing for her.

Claudette wasn't the type of woman who was impressed by good looks.

It was the man inside that impressed her.

William had such a commanding personality, such confidence, that he seemed larger than life—indestructible even when injured. Unexpectedly, he was also considerate, kind, and humorous.

What had touched her the most, though, was seeing the vulnerable side of him, which Claudette was willing to bet Agent William Kentworth didn't allow anyone else to see.

Had he let the mask slide because he trusted her not to use his vulnerability against him? Or had he done that because he had feelings for her and couldn't help himself?

How many times had he risked his life for her?

How many had he killed for her?

No one had ever done so much for Claudette.

No one.

Not even her father.

William had shown her again and again that he would do anything for her, but more than that, more than saving her life, he'd shown her a whole new way to live.

And now he was showing her a whole new way to love.

Gathering her hard and bringing her in tight to his body, his mouth found hers and as he kissed her, she felt the hard length of him pressing against her belly.

God, she wanted that with astounding desperation.

When he licked into her, his trailing fingers felt like lightning rods, drawing on her energy and taking everything she had only to return it tenfold, making her feel boneless.

"Mmm," William hummed into her mouth as he stroked a hand down her flank.

She moaned against his lips, squeezing her thighs together as she felt herself get wet.

Her core felt like it had been lit on fire, prickles of

delectable heat traveling up and spreading over her skin, electrifying, tightening, and leaving every inch tingling.

Reaching with his large hand inside her panties, he squeezed her naked butt, his one hand covering her entire bottom.

Claudette squeaked, surprised at his boldness and excited by it all at once.

He nipped her lower lip and trailed his hand back up her body, slowly sliding beneath her shirt and up her ribcage. Her breath hitched as his thumb slid up over the swell of her breast, coming to rest against her hard nipple.

When he rubbed a circle around the nub of flesh, Claudette had to close her eyes and just revel in how incredibly good it felt to be touched by him.

Why had nothing felt this way before?

She was no untested virgin, yet now a single finger rubbing her breast was enough to make her see stars.

Some of it had to be the fact that they'd been running for their lives, but she had no doubt that most of it was the effect of the man she was with.

"Lie back," William murmured.

Normally, Claudette was allergic to authority, but she obeyed William before he'd even finished speaking, settling onto her back and opening her arms in invitation.

He didn't descend on her like she'd thought he would. Instead he smiled, gently and slightly teasing, and began unbuttoning her oversized shirt.

Claudette shivered once her skin was exposed, but this time, it wasn't because she was cold. William regarded her with such lust and reverence in his eyes that she felt like a cross between a goddess and a temptress, or maybe a goddess who was a temptress.

She felt overheated by the intensity of his gaze.

"Fucking gorgeous," he said before leaning in and—

"Oh!" Claudette clapped a hand over her lips to mute her cry as William captured her nipple in his mouth.

The warmth and wetness of his tongue played havoc with her senses; she hadn't felt anything so luxuriously sinful since she'd been forced to abandon her fancy dress at the beginning of their escape. Everything had been rough, hard, something to bear but never enjoy, and being reminded of just how delicious pressure and heat could be was almost enough to make her swoon. The barest hint of his teeth made her shudder, and the urge to reach down and slip her own fingers into her panties was almost impossible to resist. She could come, just like this, with his mouth on her breast and her fingers inside her wet heat.

Lucky for her, she didn't have to use her own fingers.

His hands were so much bigger than hers but still so gentle as they quested down her body and finally cupped her mound. Claudette shuddered again.

William lifted off her. "Are you sure that you want this?"

Always the gentleman.

He really didn't have to ask at this point, but she appreciated that he had.

"Yes," she said breathlessly. "I need you."

"You've got me." He slipped a finger inside her and pressed his thumb to the throbbing bundle of nerves at the apex of her thighs.

Her vision blurring she arched her back hard. Her whole

body thrummed with electricity, every hurt of the past two days forgotten in the sudden swell of pleasure soaking through her body. "Oh, oh, o—"

William captured her mouth in a kiss just before she came, keeping her scream muffled as he slipped a second finger inside her. In moments, he brought her to another blissful orgasm that left her boneless, weightless…happy.

So goddamn happy.

"The blissful expression on your face makes me feel ten feet tall." William's voice was honey in her ear, prolonging every shiver of pleasure. "You look like everything's right with your world, like you were meant to be here, with me, and the way you feel…."

He still had his fingers inside of her, and as he pumped them gently, Claudette moaned and clenched around them.

She could go again.

38

CLAUDETTE

Claudette had experienced multiple orgasms before, but it had been a long time since she'd had more than one with a man. That sort of pleasure had just seemed out of reach. Not something to be greedy for when she could be perfectly happy with just one.

Not this time, though.

This time she wanted more, more of William, who was still dressed, and that needed to change fast.

She'd dreamt about him gloriously naked, but other than when she'd bandaged his leg, she hadn't had the pleasure of seeing him without his clothes yet.

"You're so wet." He slid a third finger inside.

Claudette watched his face as he stared down at where his fingers were pumping in and out of her, hunger in every line of his body. He wanted to be inside of her, and she wanted him there, filling her with the hard length she felt pressing against her through the fabric of his cargo pants.

Why was he holding back?

He can't actually be that much of a gentleman, can he?

Then again, if anybody in the world was ready to put her well-being before his own, it was William.

Claudette moaned softly as he moved his hand, fingers twisting as they pressed in and out of her body. "I want you," she said. "I want you inside of me."

"Hmm." William grinned at her. "I know, darling. But I need to prepare you first."

There was no way he thought she was a virgin, and he was still concerned about her level of readiness after she'd climaxed twice?

She swallowed hard. "How big are you?"

"Big enough that three fingers are a good idea, luv. Trust me."

"I do," she said, her voice breaking on the second word as he sped up. "I do, I do, please, just—I want you now, I want you inside of me…fuck me, fuck me."

"Shite," William expelled, pulling his fingers out just as she was about to climax for the third time.

Claudette was sure she'd get right back to it, though, and seeing William finally undress was well worth the momentary frustration.

She watched him fumble with his shirt as he rushed to take it off, and when his muscular chest was finally revealed, she licked her lips, eager for the rest of his clothing to come off.

He reared up on his knees and shoved his pants down, and when he pulled out his shaft a moment later—

Oh. Oh, holy hell.

Her eyes widened as lust mingled with apprehension. He

really was big. Most men said that and left a girl wondering whether they were myopic, but not William. Claudette had to admit he was right. Three fingers was a good idea. Maybe even four, but first...

"Lie down," she said, her mouth watering at the thought of wrapping her lips around that bulging head.

She scooted over enough that he had space, then rolled over and crouched between his legs.

"Claudette." He sounded pained as he reached with his hand to cup her cheek. "You don't have to—"

"I want to," she said.

Giving blowjobs was something she was good at and, more importantly, enjoyed. She could do this—she wanted to get him revved up the same way he'd done for her.

"Are you sure?" William caressed her cheek, his eyes full of lust and something else she didn't dare name.

"Don't worry." Claudette swallowed as she reached out and stroked along his shaft. "I won't choke."

"Oh, fucking—" Whatever else he was going to say was lost to a groan as she wrapped her lips around the bulbous head and slowly, slickly lowered her mouth down as far as it could comfortably go.

Which wasn't all that far, but that was fine.

There was nothing less sexy than choking in the middle of a blowjob unless the other person went for that sort of thing.

Right now, all she wanted was to make William feel good. Judging by the way his eyes were fluttering closed, mouth slack as she kitten-licked his slit before sliding down again, she was doing a good job of that.

You haven't felt anything yet, darling.

Claudette got more comfortable on her knees, spreading her thighs to give her a broader base of support, then focused all her attention on William and his delicious, thick length. She used one hand to stroke the base of his shaft, occasionally lowering her lips far enough to meet the top of her fist before sliding back up. The other hand went to his balls, pulling them gently, rolling them in her hand, and scratching her nails along them.

He particularly seemed to like that.

"Fuck, fuck," he chanted.

Yes, that would come soon, but Claudette hadn't gotten enough of this yet, not even close. Moving her head up and down, she closed her eyes and lost herself in the sensation of sucking, licking, and pumping with her hand.

He was so hard, so hot between her lips. When the lightest coat of pre-come formed at the tip, letting her know he was getting closer, she pulled her head off and watched a crystal-clear drop form, then slowly slide down the side of his cock until it hit her hand. She leaned in and licked it off.

"God." William suddenly reached out and grabbed her, pulling her away from her prize and further up his body. He crushed their lips together, holding her tight enough to take her breath away.

Claudette loved it, reveled in the fact that she'd finally made him lose control.

"Do it now," she whispered when he finally pulled back. "Fuck me now."

39

CLAUDETTE

With a sexy smirk, William put his hands on Claudette's hips. "You're the one on top, darling." He circled his hands to squeeze her butt cheeks. "If you want it? All you have to do is take it."

He was right.

Sometime during their frenzied make-out session, she'd crawled all the way up until she was straddling his waist.

That wasn't what Claudette had in mind when she'd begged him to fuck her, but she could play this game he seemed to be enjoying so much.

They had both been tested and were clean, and she was on birth control, so there was no reason to worry about protection. She was free to do as she pleased with this incredible man, and she intended to do it all.

Lightly scratching a hand down William's chest, she enjoyed the way it made him squirm a little. "I think I will."

She scooted back until his erection was flush with her ass.

As she began to rub herself against him, coating his shaft with her juices and luxuriating in the feeling of how big he was, she let her eyes drift closed.

Slowly, she inched higher and higher until the head was at her entrance and then paused. Her eyes flying open, she held her breath for a moment before lowering herself just enough for him to breach the tight ring of muscles of her sheath.

William panted, his fingers digging painfully into her hips as he held himself still. She was torturing him by allowing only the tip to breach her entrance, and he was struggling not to ram up into her.

Mostly, she did it to prolong the pleasure and build up the anticipation, but admittedly, a small part of her wondered if he would fit comfortably inside of her.

Claudette managed to hold off for a few seconds until the need to complete the joining became undeniable, then slowly, deliberately, she began lowering herself on his shaft.

Oh God. Oh God, she felt so full, and she hadn't taken even a quarter of him in.

She was slippery to the point that her thighs were glistening, yet it hardly seemed like enough now that she was taking him inside her.

Fuck, he was big, and the stretching sensation was delicious with just a hint of pain to enhance the pleasure.

When William added his fingers to the play, circling the sensitive bundle of nerves at the front of her opening, the slickening of her sheath was enough to allow her to lower herself the last few inches down and join them completely.

The stretching sensation was incredible, not painful but

not comfortable either. She'd never had a lover that large, and she needed a moment to adjust before she could start moving.

Touching her lower belly, Claudette was half convinced that she'd be able to feel him there if she shifted just a little bit.

"You're amazing," William murmured hoarsely.

His eyes were locked on her face, and his fingers gripped her hips, holding her in place.

"Give me a moment," she said, a little breathless. "Just a moment...."

"Take all the time you need." His eyes never veered away from hers.

When she was finally ready to start moving, she did so hesitantly, just a shift of her hips back and forth. At first, she did lean forward a little so that she could rub her clit on his abs, and when that felt good, her small grinds got longer and larger until finally, she was riding up and down so far that he nearly fell out of her before she glided back down.

Every inch of him lit a spark inside her, filling her with more than his body.

It felt perfect.

No one had ever satisfied her so completely while doing nothing more than letting her take control.

It wasn't easy for him, she could read it in the hard line of his lips and the tight muscles of his jaw, but he was letting her lead because he cared and knew that she needed it.

She could come, just like this, she could come, and it would be—

William reached up and squeezed her nipples in between

his fingers, hard, and Claudette bit back a shriek as a bolt of lightning seemed to snap between her breasts and her core.

"More." She moved a hand down to her clit and thrummed it quickly between her fingers. "Fuck, yes, yes, oh!"

She sat down hard, squeezing his shaft so tight that she could feel him flex in response.

The waves didn't roll through her this time; they crushed her, and as the climax overwhelmed her senses, it took every shred of focus she had left not to scream William's name at the top of her lungs.

40

CLAUDETTE

Claudette collapsed on William's chest, her cheek landing right over his heart, which was thundering in sync with hers.

With his warm breath wafting over her forehead and the small hairs on his chest tickling her over-sensitized nipples, she'd never felt closer to a man and wished it would never end.

Wrapping an arm around her waist, he flipped them over without severing the connection below.

On her back, impaled on his thick shaft, languorous with pleasure and still feeling the aftershocks of her orgasm, Claudette could do nothing more than spread her legs wide and let William chase what he needed.

Apparently, what he needed was to fuck her like a beast.

Lifting her legs, he put them over his shoulders, so she was spread out for him so completely it would have been embarrassing if she had the energy to care.

Soon, she could think of nothing other than him moving

hard and fast inside of her, every drag lighting her senses up anew as he worked toward his own orgasm.

His balls slapped her ass as he thrust, the wet sounds of them coming together lewd in what was otherwise such quiet, still surroundings.

He fucked her, and kept fucking her until, to her immense surprise, Claudette found her body rising to the occasion again.

"Oh, my God."

William laughed breathlessly. "I knew I could get you up there again."

"I can't... I've never..."

"You can do it. Touch yourself," he ordered.

Claudette obeyed immediately, pinching her nipples hard.

It felt so good, just a little jolt of bright, sharp pain to accent the pleasure.

Hell, she was going to come again, and she was buying herself a set of nipple clamps first thing when she got home because until now, she had no idea playing with them like this would affect her like that.

Then again, maybe it was more the man she was with than the act itself. She left one hand on her breast as the other trailed back down to her clit. She was so sensitive there now, all she could do was set her fingers on either side of it and give a little pressure.

That was enough, though. "I'm going to come again," she said.

William shuddered.

"I'm almost there. Come with me this time. In me. I want you to. I want to feel it."

He thrust two, three more times and then ground in as hard as he could, mouth falling open and eyes closing as he came.

Claudette increased the pressure on her clit just a smidgen, and there it was, a gentle orgasm this time, just a cresting wave, but it was still wonderful and bright enough to leave her glassy-eyed and full of wonder.

The air smelled like sweat, like sex, like them. She loved it.

She loved him.

William didn't pull out like she thought he would. Instead, he lowered himself on top of her and drew her into another kiss. His tenderness after the fact was enough to make her feel giddy.

After this, no one could ever live up to her expectations.

Hell, she didn't want anyone else after this.

Was it possible for a thief and a spy to build a future together?

"William," she whispered.

He went still, sensing that she had something important to say.

"I...I want..."

How did you tell a spy that you wanted something real with him?

How did you tell him that you thought you'd fallen in love with him?

All I can do is be honest. Everything else can be worked out later, even if it means picking up the pieces of my broken heart alone.

"William, I—" She suddenly stopped as the sound of a helicopter registered. "Is that…"

"Yeah." He smiled ruefully. "That's our ride. Time to get out of here, darling."

No! It was too soon. She needed a few more moments.

MARIAN WOKE UP.

41

MARCUS

Marcus woke with a start.

He'd been warned that coming out of the session might be disorienting at first, but that was a massive understatement.

One moment he'd been making love to an amazing woman, and the next, he was reclining in a chair with a harsh light glaring overhead, and an IV had just been removed from his arm.

He felt as if he'd been destroyed, rebuilt from the ground up, and destroyed again upon waking.

He didn't want to be back in reality.

He wanted to return to the virtual world and reunite with Claudette, the best woman he'd ever met, the best lover, the best everything.

"Good evening, sir." His technician smiled at him from where he was pressing a cotton ball to where the needle had been. "Did you have an enjoyable experience?"

"I..." Enjoyable didn't really seem to cover it. "It was

amazing." Especially at the end. "Oh, shit!" He glanced down at his groin and was relieved to see that he wasn't sporting a hard-on in front of the tech, who kindly ignored his sudden jolt and pressed a Band-Aid to his elbow.

"I'm glad to hear that," the tech said. "All client reviews give us helpful information when it comes to designing new adventures, but positive ones are especially nice to hear. Take your time getting up. Your experience coordinator will be waiting in the hallway to escort you out whenever you're ready." He left the room, and Marcus took a moment to just stare up at the ceiling and breathe.

All the minor aches and pains he'd felt as William were gone, and now he knew them to be minor by comparison to how bad they should have felt.

The gash in his leg especially.

But the same could be true about the ecstasy he'd experienced with Claudette.

Claudette.

It hadn't been real.

She hadn't really been there.

Marcus closed his eyes and tried to pull her image up in his mind, but already the details were fading. Bright eyes, long legs, long hair, that laugh of hers that could spear through his heart, the way she felt in his arms, on his shaft.

Fuck, and now he was getting hard.

"You wanted to be a super spy," he muttered to himself as he rubbed a hand down his face. "You sure as hell got what you asked for."

Right down to getting the girl.

The spy experience he'd been after had been amazing—

the adrenaline rush, the danger so narrowly avoided—but that wasn't what had stuck with him.

It was the woman.

Because she was real.

Whoever had been playing Claudette was a real person, someone who'd wanted an adventure of her own as a high-end, daring jewel thief. No wonder she was the most memorable part of the experience.

What was she like in real life?

No. Don't go there. That's not what you came here for.

He didn't want the complications that came with dating and had paid a substantial amount to enjoy spending time with an amazing woman while avoiding all the pitfalls of dating in the real world.

He didn't regret a moment of it, and it had been worth every penny. In the span of three hours, he'd lived over a month as William the spy, and it had been incredible despite being difficult and, at times, excruciating.

Marcus would do it all again in a heartbeat and without batting an eyelid at the price tag.

Taking a deep breath, he got to his feet and walked over to the chair where the tech had left his jacket and tie. He put them on, once more adopting the persona of Marcus Shurman, corporate shark, instead of William Kentworth, secret agent.

So that was it.

It was over.

He'd done it, it had been everything he'd hoped and more, and now he could return to his everyday life feeling refreshed.

Fine. Good. Great.

Except, the man leaving the room wasn't the same as the man who had entered it.

He'd been forever changed by the experience.

By her.

With a sigh, Marcus walked over to the door and opened it.

His experience coordinator was there to greet him with a set smile. "Mr. Shurman," she began, "our technician assures me you had a pleasant experience! I hope that we were able to meet your needs and—"

"I want to do it again."

They both blinked.

Marcus would have sworn that he hadn't even considered asking for another round, but apparently, he could still surprise himself.

"Oh!" Her smile became more natural. "Well, of course we can do that!"

Farther down the hall, another technician stepped out of a room.

Was that Claudette's room?

Was the woman he'd shared this incredible experience with there right now?

If he were to walk in there, who would he see?

Was she anything like her avatar or nothing like it at all?

Did it even matter after the time they'd had together?

"And I'd like it to be with the same person, if possible," he added.

"Ah." His coordinator nodded. "That's certainly possible, provided that your partner is so inclined. Naturally, we will inform her of your preferences and let her decide whether she wants to join you on another adventure. In case she doesn't, do you have a timespan in mind before we start looking for a different partner for you?"

"I only want her, and as for the time span, it's unlimited."

"Um…"

"Anytime she wants back in," Marcus said, knowing he was probably coming off a bit desperate but unable to help it. "And in case her finances don't allow it, I'll gladly pay for her token as well." He smiled. "Your AI did an amazing job matching me with the perfect woman. I can't imagine getting so lucky again."

"Thank you." Lesley, the experience coordinator, gave him a knowing smile. "I'm glad you enjoyed your adventure as well as your partner."

"I did, and if you can let her know that, I'll appreciate it."

Perhaps if Claudette knew how much he'd enjoyed being with her, she would be more amenable to joining him for another adventure.

"Certainly, Mr. Shurman." Lesley inclined her head. "Since you had such a good time, perhaps you can leave a review on our website. The more positive reviews we get, the less hesitant people are about giving our service a chance."

"I'll do it as soon as I get home. Reading the reviews helped me decide to go on a virtual adventure and have the best time of my life. The decent thing to do is to pay it forward."

"Indeed." Lesley escorted him to the front door and shook his hand.

It was almost nine at night—the perfect time to get ready to go out if he wanted to head out to the clubs, but he didn't.

Nothing he could imagine out there felt tempting.

Don't be stupid and fall in love with someone who doesn't exist.

He wasn't really in love.

Marcus had been warned that emotions could linger after the experience, but he'd also been told that they always dissipate before long. He was still riding the high of what he'd been through. It would wane, and he would go back to normal.

Except, he didn't want to go back to his old life.

Normal was boring nights and repetitive days, normal was meetings in high-rises and handling financial crises. Normal was women whose names he never remembered. Normal wasn't enough.

Hopefully, whoever Claudette was, she wasn't satisfied with the ordinary either.

42

MARCUS

Marcus slept solidly that night and woke up ready for his workout in the morning.

On weekends, his sessions with Doug were twice as long because he didn't have to go to the office, and his trainer showed him no mercy for the same reason. But Marcus was still so pumped up that he managed to tap Doug out twice during their sparring, which had never happened before.

Doug, of course, was all smiles about it.

"Either you had a wonderful time with someone last night, or you got a great night's sleep," he said with a laugh after getting out of Marcus's chokehold. "Or both."

"Option B," Marcus said.

Doug sat back on the mat and looked at him. "Oh hey, you had your experience yesterday, huh?"

"I did."

Doug's smile turned knowing. "Tuckered you out, I guess."

Marcus smiled back. "Something like that." He didn't

really want to talk about it. It still felt private, special. Intimate.

Luckily, Doug knew when not to push. Verbally, at least. "I'm glad it worked out for you, man," he said. "Now prepare to cry for your mama." He tapped Marcus three times in under a minute, and they finished the session grinning.

Marcus knew better than to expect to hear about another experience soon. After all, the first one had taken weeks to set up. If the next one took another few weeks, well, as long as it was the same partner, it would be worth it. He was prepared to be patient.

When Lesley called that same afternoon, Marcus was pleasantly surprised.

"Mr. Shurman!" Her voice was bubbly with excitement. "I hope you're having a good day so far!"

"I have the feeling it's about to get better," he said, a surge of anticipation making his fingertips tingle.

"It is! It turns out your partner enjoyed the adventure as much as you did, and she would like to arrange another one at your earliest convenience. She included a list of potential—"

"How's tonight?" Marcus asked.

The previous experience had taken a long time to set up because it required a lot of customization, but this time, he wasn't going to be picky.

He would take whatever generic, ready-made adventure they could offer him.

His coordinator laughed. "You haven't even heard the list of future experiences your partner is interested in!"

"I'm not picky. As long as she is in the adventure, I don't

care what scenario is playing. If she wants to be Cinderella, I'll be Prince Charming, and if she wants to be Belle, I'll be the beast. I'm flexible."

It was good that he was home and no one from his office had heard him say that because they would have called him out on his lie. Marcus had a well-earned reputation for being regimented and obdurate.

"I'll send them to you to peruse. Take your time looking them over," she advised. "We want every experience to stand on its own. We don't recommend trying to rebuild the last one you had—that tends to lead to disappointment. If you and your partner choose one of the ready-made adventures, the earliest we can schedule a session for you is Monday at seven in the evening. Will that work for you?"

"Perfect."

Marcus was more than excited about another adventure, he was so damn happy that it worried him. Just thinking about being with her put a stupid smile on his face that he couldn't get rid of.

He wasn't that guy. Or was he?

The old Marcus Shurman was a well-oiled machine, goal-oriented, and unfeeling. But right now, he couldn't care less about the stock market or how much his portfolio had grown.

In fact, he was tempted to call in sick on Monday and spend the day preparing for his adventure, and that was coming from a guy who hadn't taken a day off in over two years.

He was losing it. Losing himself in the fantasy he had created, and he couldn't allow himself to do that.

He had to be more careful with his heart.

Maybe this second time would break the spell and show him that it really was the experience that had done it for him rather than the person he'd shared it with.

Yeah. It would be worth it just to know that much.

43

MARCUS

Monday couldn't come soon enough. Marcus was already loosening his tie as he entered Perfect Match's office, and he greeted his experience coordinator with a friendly nod instead of the grimace he knew he'd been wearing when he walked into this place for the first time.

"Mr. Shurman!" She shook his hand. "All ready for your undersea adventure?"

"All ready," he said as she led the way back.

Out of the experiences his partner had selected for him to peruse, he'd chosen the one he was least likely to enjoy. He had to know whether the effect the previous adventure had on him resulted from the scenario he'd chosen or the woman who had agreed to share it with him.

He had a feeling it was the woman, his Claudette, but after this session, he would know for sure. If the experience proved to be as exceptional as the previous one despite the strange and unappealing environment, then it was all her.

"Excellent," Lesley said with a smile. "You didn't indicate any issues with water, phobias, or the like, but you might not be aware of them. I want to remind you that this experience is designed to take place entirely underwater. You'll be given the form of a being that can handle the environment, and it should feel effortless to be in the depths of the ocean, but if for some reason you begin to experience significant distress, we'll, of course, wake you up. Your technician will closely monitor your body's responses throughout the adventure, so you can be assured that we will not let any harm come to you."

"Of course. I read the instructions carefully and know exactly what to expect."

"Perfect." She indicated the familiar chair to him, then helped him out of his jacket and hung it on the back of the same chair as before. "You and your partner are scheduled for the usual three hours, which should equate to a bit over a day inside this particular experience. Does everything sound acceptable to you?"

He wasn't happy about the short duration, but given that he wasn't particularly enthused about an underwater adventure, perhaps it was for the best. He could always schedule another session, and now that he knew that his partner was as ready to play as he was, he was no longer anxious about her refusing to do it again.

Except, this time, he wouldn't be partnered with Claudette. She would have a different name and a different avatar.

"My partner." He stumbled a little over the word but pressed on. "How will I recognize her if we're going to look different this time than we did before?"

Lesley smiled knowingly. "Oh, you'll know her, Mr. Shurman. Please." She indicated the chair again. "Sit down and get comfortable. Your technician is on his way."

"Thank you." He sat back and stared at the wall, his mind racing even as he tried to control his heartbeat. It was going to be okay. He knew that much. The experience last time had been incredible, and he'd yet to read a bad review about this place.

But what if it wasn't the same? What if *she* wasn't the same? What if the chemistry they'd managed to create together couldn't be recreated in a different adventure?

You can't capture lightning in a bottle.

If once was all there was, then he'd know after this session was over. And if somehow they managed to have anywhere close to the fun and excitement they had during the previous session, then it would really be something special.

The sex had been phenomenal last time, but he could get that anywhere. A partner to go on a genuine adventure with him, however, someone who fit him in more ways than he thought was possible, that was much more difficult to find.

"Good evening, Mr. Shurman," the technician greeted him as he shut the door. "Are you ready to begin?"

He rolled up the sleeve on his right arm. "I'm ready."

"What is your avatar's name?"

"Gilean."

It took a few minutes to go over the safety protocol, a

few more to get him hooked up, then another minute to make sure his partner was in the experience as well, and then, it was lights out.

44

MARCUS/GILEAN

Gilean looked over at his mate, and his heart filled with pride.

Holding her trident firmly in one hand and a net coiled loosely around the other arm, Thalesse looked magnificent. Most of her long green hair was tied back, but a few loose pieces floated around her face, and he fought the urge to tuck them into her braid.

Their people were watching, though, and they were supposed to look fierce and determined, not tender and loving.

But how could he feel anything else?

In the bright light of the lagoon, the scales of Thalesse's tail shimmered bright red, and her eyes glowed with resolve.

She was the most beautiful mer in the seven oceans, and if anyone dared to claim otherwise, they would have to defend that claim to the death.

"Are you ready for this?" she murmured.

"Of course I am." He hefted his trident, resetting his grip closer to the three-pronged head.

The moment they left the lagoon, they would begin their trial for command—hunting one of the massive, thirty-foot-long sharks that swam these waters, taking it down together, and bringing it back as a tribute to their king and queen.

Doing so would prove their worthiness as future rulers of the sea people.

They weren't the only contenders, though. Two other couples were competing. One of them they were friendly with, and Gilean anticipated a healthy amount of competition from them. Not enough for them to win, but it would be fun while it lasted.

The other couple, though...

He and Samar had been rivals since they were young, fighting with tooth and fin as children and, later, net and trident. Only direct intervention from the king had kept them from dueling to the death.

Mating Thalesse had changed Gilean and made him realize there was more to life than triumph in battle, but he had the feeling that Samar was still thirsty for blood. If he and his mate, Ravelle, somehow ambushed them out in open waters...if they cut them while they were out among the sharks...things could turn nasty, fast.

He would never let anything bad happen to Thalesse, and he knew that she felt the same about him. They would look after each other and woe to any who tried to come between them or cause either of them harm.

As the horn sounded, Gilean swam forward, picking up

speed so that he would be able to leap over the thin strand of reef that separated the lagoon from the greater ocean. Thalesse kept pace effortlessly.

Just before they reached the point where they would need to jump, he glanced over at her. Her grin was fierce, her face full of determination and joy.

Joy.

She was his joy, and he would never forget that.

They leaped together out into the vast, dark ocean, and into the adventure of a lifetime...

On their third adventure, they flew into the unknown together, leading their colony ship to a new planet that would hopefully prove a better, kinder place than the world they'd just escaped from...

On the fourth, he and his partner danced late into the night, the jazz finally subsiding from the frantic beats of earlier in the night into something soft and slow now that the floor was nearly abandoned...

During their fifth, they nestled close together behind locked doors, Secret Service in place as they let their adrenaline from the attempted assassination of the President of the United States and his wife slowly fade away...

. . .

On the sixth, they settled onto matching lounge chairs on the pure white, sandy beach, holding hands and sipping colorful cocktails as they relaxed in the warm sunshine, with the distant chirping of a tropical bird the only sound to accompany the gentle roll of the surf.

It was perfect...

All their adventures had been perfect.

If there was one sure thing that Marcus could take away from the experiences that he was now booking twice a week with his still-anonymous partner, it was that each experience gave him precisely what he needed. And what he needed, more than any setting or scenario, more than adrenaline or adventure, was the person he was having these adventures with.

He had to know more about her. His Claudette, his Thalesse, his Jocelyn, his Diana—different names, different looks, but the same person underneath it all. The intelligence, humor, and passion didn't change along with the avatars.

He had to find out if it felt the same for her, if he sparked the same level of desire and intrigue that he felt whenever he thought about her.

45

MARIAN

Marian felt amazing stepping into her apartment. Her whole body still tingled with the aftereffects of her latest experience, the most romantic she'd had so far.

Her partner had suggested they tour Venice this time around, and she'd agreed—why not? She'd never been, and with the way work was constantly piling up, she might never be able to carve out enough vacation time to get to the real place.

The trip had been amazing. It had felt like three full days of Venetian extravagance, with private tours of the most beautiful museums and dining in incredible restaurants, not to mention the gondola ride they'd had right before returning to their suite and ending the night in a very memorable fashion.

Marian laughed out loud, giving herself permission to turn in a little circle in her foyer before she removed her heels and set them on the shoe rack. Whoever her partner was, the man was the most incredible lover she'd ever had, and his performance had remained consistent in all their different experiences.

Not that she was a slouch, the way he'd responded to her touch this last time had proven that, but—

Her phone buzzed. Marian sighed and checked the caller.

Gigi. Again.

She'd been avoiding the woman for the past two days, tired of constantly being called on to be more than her lawyer. Didn't Gigi have any friends left?

Marian let the call ring through. She felt a bit guilty about it, but she hadn't even had dinner yet. Clients could wait until her stomach wasn't rumbling anymore. Her taste buds primed for Italian food, she pulled up the website for her favorite local restaurant and ordered a serving of their risotto all'Amarone before heading into her bedroom.

Undressing slowly, she pressed her hands in all the same places her partner's had been pressed not so long ago—or, at least, had felt like they were pressed.

It dampened her mood a bit to remember that none of it had been real. While her mind was enjoying the entire range of human emotions and experiences, her body was just lying there in a chair, inert.

How wonderful it would be to have a real person touch her the way her partner in the experiences had. It had felt so authentic while it was happening, but something was missing upon waking up in the real world.

Marian lay back on her bed and slowly ran her hands down her freshly-revealed leg, tracing a line from her knee up the inside of her thigh. It felt good, but having him touch her was so much better. Wouldn't it be wonderful to have it every night instead of twice a week?

It was such a decadent indulgence, and even with how much she was making, Marian couldn't continue booking sessions like they were giving them out for free.

You can have it all if you agree to meet the guy in the real world.

I can't.

Marian was never going to actually meet this mystery partner of hers, no matter how much she was tempted to do so. It would ruin the one good thing she had going on right now. There was just no way he was as amazing in real life, and once the illusion was shattered, it could never be the same.

Bzzt. Bzzt. Bzzt.

Shit.

Knowing that Gigi just wasn't going to quit at this point, Marian sighed and got up to get her phone. "Hello," she answered, the last of the high from her experience draining away as Gigi's upset voice filled her ear.

"He sold the boat!" she wailed. "That son of a bitch sold the boat! I wanted it, he knew I wanted it, I always loved it more than he did, and now he's sold it, and I'll never see it again!"

"Gigi." Marian kept her voice calm out of sheer force of will. "You'll get your fair share from the proceeds, you know that."

"It's not about a fair share! It's about getting what's mine, and that boat was mine!"

"The legal documentation said otherwise."

"Screw the legal documentation," Gigi said viciously. "You're the one who has to give a damn about that stuff, not me! You told me you'd get me that boat, and now he's gone and sold it, and I'll never get it! This is your fault. I can't believe I trusted you on top of—"

A switch went off inside Marian.

She'd just spent what felt like three days being adored by the man of her dreams. She wasn't going to sacrifice all the benefits that had brought her, mental and emotional, by listening to her sad and unhinged client abuse her. "Ms. Webb, I suggest you stop right there."

Taken by surprise, Gigi actually did what Marian had asked.

Buoyed by the immediate compliance, Marian continued in a stern voice. "I never once told you I would be able to get you that boat. You stated you wanted it, and I assured you I would get you everything you're entitled to. The fact of the matter is, the boat was in your husband's name. He held the title. Even though you're currently going through a divorce, he's within his rights to sell it as long as he did so for a fair price. I will ensure that he did. What I won't do is allow you to accuse me of malpractice. I've allowed you far more freedom with communication than most lawyers would, partly because I feel sorry about your circumstances. I'm committed to getting you the best deal possible from your divorce proceedings, but I will not allow my practice or my ethics to come under fire without cause. If you want to file a formal complaint against me, you can do so, but be aware that I'll defend myself vigorously. If you file a complaint against me, our client/attorney relationship would obviously end."

"I...I...Marian, I never intended to question your ethics, I...."

"Good," she said. "Then I suggest you end this call and make an appointment with a professional therapist who is better equipped to handle your current emotional crisis. It's not my job, and it's not something I'm interested in listening to from here on out. I am your lawyer, first and foremost. Not your relationship counselor."

"What about a friend?" Gigi asked timidly.

Marian sighed. "Maybe once your case is over. Until then, you need to let me work and only communicate with me on a professional basis. Otherwise, I can recommend several other excellent divorce attorneys to you."

"No, no! I...all right, I'm...hanging up now."

"Goodnight, Ms. Webb." Marian ended the call and stared at the phone in her hand. She felt somewhere between elated and deeply disturbed by her actions.

What had happened to her? Had she been so changed by the experiences that it had started to affect her work?

Was she sorry, though?

Not in the slightest.

46

MARIAN

Marian never spoke to clients like that. Her soft touch was one of her selling points, and it counterbalanced her barracuda reputation. Her clientele wanted an attorney to hold their hands while aggressively negotiating the best settlement for them.

That was why they were willing to pay her top-dollar fees.

If word got out that she was rude to her clients or that she didn't have patience for them, her practice would suffer.

Then again, she had to draw the line somewhere, and Gigi had overstepped her bounds and then some. If she decided to drop Marian as her attorney, it would be a shame, but it wouldn't be a huge loss.

Marian had plenty of cases humming along that would cover her expenses very nicely without also digging their claws into her limited free time.

The question was how deeply offended Gigi felt. The woman was well-connected, and if she decided to go on a smear campaign against Marian, that could create a problem in the long term.

It wasn't likely, though.

As her phone signaled an incoming message, she inhaled deeply.

I swear to God, Gigi, if this is you... or maybe I should use the opportunity to soften the blow and be nice to her.

But it wasn't her. It was an unknown number and a disturbingly unexpected message.

Hi, Marian. You don't know me, not in person anyway. My name is Marcus Shurman, and I'm the guy who's been partnering with you in the Perfect Match adventures.

Marian sat abruptly on the floor. Was this even legal?

She'd read over the contract with the care of the professional she was, and there had been no loopholes in the privacy and anonymity clauses. The only way Marcus Shurman could have contacted her was through Perfect Match.

Had he been stalking her?

How had he figured out who she was?

Had he bribed the tech or the experience coordinator to reveal her information? Or had he paid someone to hack into the Perfect Match database and pluck out her name?

Hell, he could be a hacker himself for all she knew, and in any case, this was stalker behavior, and it scared her.

Now that he had her name and phone number, finding out where she lived would be a piece of cake.

Another message arrived immediately on the heels of the previous one.

I don't mean to scare you. I only learned who you are after tonight's Experience when I happened to catch sight of your license plate as you drove out of the parking lot. Yours was the only other car leaving at the same time I was.

God, she should never have gotten a vanity plate with her damn company name on it.

I've been curious about meeting you for a while, so I decided to reach out. Rest assured, I have no intention of making this weird.

Ha, it was too late for that.

But after her initial mini-panic attack, Marian reminded herself of the many hours she'd spent with this man. True, she'd only met his avatar, but the mind driving the experience belonged to Marcus Shurman, and there was no way that the man she'd gotten to know so well meant her harm.

Through all the adventures, in all of his different guises, he'd been a gentleman—considerate, polite, and always putting her needs ahead of his own.

Besides, her curiosity was piqued, and she wanted to find out more about him.

Marian kept on reading.

If you never want to meet me in person, I completely understand. I know that's not how I should have handled this. I should have gone through Perfect Match to get your approval, but up until today, I was sure that meeting you in the Experiences was enough and that I didn't want anything more. But I was lying to myself. I haven't been able to stop thinking about you, and when I saw that license plate, I perceived it as a sign and decided to act on it. If you prefer we limit our interactions to Experiences, I respect that, but I'd really love to meet you in person.

Feel free to research me as well. Again, if you're not interested in this, all you have to do is text back 'No,' and I'll never reach out again. I do hope this doesn't discourage you from more Experiences with me in the future, though. Thank you, and thanks for a great trip to Venice.

The message ended with a web address.

Marian stared at her phone in disbelief. There was no way she was meeting Marcus Shurman in person, but she was definitely going to find out everything she could about him.

47

MARIAN

A wine glass in her hand and a laptop braced on a pillow, Marian leaned back against the couch pillows and typed in the web address Marcus had texted her.

She hesitated with her finger hovering over the go button.

What if he was painfully ugly or decades older than her?

If the guy wasn't at least average-looking and age-appropriate, it might ruin the fantasy for her.

Or maybe not.

After all, going in, she wouldn't know that she was inside a virtual fantasy and that the man behind her handsome love interest wasn't as sexy in the real world. The problem was what would happen once she was back to reality.

Her memories of the adventure would be tainted, and the pleasant afterglow she enjoyed coming out of the experience would fizzle out.

Then again, would Marcus have given her his information if he feared she would be disappointed with what he really looked like?

Probably not.

Biting her lower lip, Marian hit enter and held her breath.

What came up was an investment company's home page, along with a list of founding partners. Right at the top was Marcus Shurman, along with his picture.

He...holy shit.

Holy freaking shit!

Was that picture even real, or had he Photoshopped the hell out of it?

She'd been on a couple of dates with men who'd used a picture of a model on their dating profile. Perhaps Marcus Shurman had done the same.

People in the real world didn't look like that, and that was doubly true for investment portfolio managers.

Maybe she could find more pictures of him together with his partners or at some company function. He wouldn't have been able to alter those as well, would he?

Clicking around, she found to her dismay that Marcus Shurman was really as good-looking as he appeared in his headshot. In one picture, he stood between a diminutive older lady and another man, towering over both. If not for the second guy, Marian would have thought that the older woman was tiny.

Great, so he had a great body in addition to a face that belonged on a movie poster.

Then she found him in another picture, holding a champagne glass at an office Christmas party and looking just as amazing as in the other two.

Damn.

Marian closed her eyes and exhaled.

She had no business with Marcus Shurman.

She considered herself a little above-average looking, but she wasn't anywhere near his league. A guy like him should be dating movie stars and supermodels.

Then again, if he'd found her by looking up her firm's name, he must have also found out what she looked like. Her firm didn't post headshots of the partners or the staff, and she kept her social media accounts private, but with a minimal effort, he could have found her picture somewhere.

The guy wouldn't have reached out without checking whether she was worth the trouble. Surprisingly, he must have decided that she was.

It was flattering, but it didn't mean that she had to reciprocate.

Damn it, she'd been perfectly happy with meeting him in the virtual world. Why did he have to ruin it?

Marian had opted for the Perfect Match solution to avoid the complications of real-life relationships, and here was this stupidly handsome man who was incredibly fun and adventurous—at least in their experiences—reaching out to her for a meeting.

Was he deluding himself thinking that they could have something better in real life?

Marian lifted her phone, pulled up the messages application, and typed *No*. She was just about to hit send when her doorbell rang.

Oh shit! Had he come to her house?

Or was it Gigi, drunk and ready to slap her the minute she opened the door!

Or—

A new notification came in on her phone. *Your order has arrived*!

Or it was her dinner? Marian pressed a hand to her chest for a moment, then got to her feet and went to retrieve her meal.

She didn't send her message to Marcus before doing so, and she didn't send it while eating her delicious dinner, either.

Her excuse was that it was crass to text and eat at the same time. Besides, it would be rude to answer with just a no. She needed to come up with a nice way to say it without coming off like something an attorney had written.

She would send it off once she was done with dinner.

After rinsing the dishes.

After putting them in the dishwasher.

She still hadn't texted him back by the time she climbed into bed.

Her phone rested on the nightstand, looking much larger and more ominous than it should.

It was discourteous to keep Marcus waiting, but she still didn't know what to say to him other than no. Given that putting down words on paper or a computer screen was what she did for a living, the problem wasn't her inability to express herself coherently in writing.

What if this really was a chance at something great?

For just a moment, Marian put her skepticism aside, lowered her shields, and allowed herself to hope.

What if fear was keeping her from having a shot at something real?

What if she could make a life with Marcus Shurman?

They could have such smart and gorgeous children together...

Right.

Marian's defenses slammed back down, and her skepticism returned with a vengeance.

She didn't really know the guy. He'd been amazing in all their fantasy worlds, but she hadn't seen him smiling in any of the photos on his company's website.

In fact, he looked stiff, stern, and conceited.

Then again, people who met her in the courtroom or across the negotiation table probably didn't have a very favorable impression of her either. The woman, or female, Marcus had shared all those wonderful experiences with, hadn't been the real Marian. It was the best version of her, the one she would have shown the world if she hadn't lost faith in people, didn't have to earn a living while swimming in shark-infested waters, as if she was fearless.

The same was probably true of Marcus Shurman. The guy she'd met in the Perfect Match experiences was his alter ego, the man he wanted to be if everything was right in his world.

He was an investment fund manager, a very successful one, and guys like him had a reputation for being ruthless and cerebral. Kindness, chivalry, and selflessness were not the words typically associated with them.

Right.

Now she was letting the pendulum swing all the way to the other end. Next, she would start imagining skeletons in his closet, axes in the trunk of his car, erectile dysfunction, or some other crippling disease.

Realistically, everyone had something, including Marcus Shurman. He might look like a god, but he was just a man.

Maybe he was a stutterer?

Or painfully shy?

She wouldn't mind the last two. In fact, it would make him seem more human and approachable.

Marian groaned. Why did he have to be so damn hot?

Yeah, fine, so she was a bit shallow, and his good looks affected her more than they should, but she was experienced enough to know that surface attraction meant nothing.

She'd seen it too many times—clients who married the man or woman of their dreams, not a hair out of place, yet who turned out to be terrible people who wouldn't piss on you if you were on fire.

She didn't want to risk that for herself and suffer the heartbreak that was sure to follow.

Yeah, great.

Her risk aversion was a sure way to realize a life of loneliness because, at this rate, she would never find anyone she deemed worthy of taking a risk on.

She didn't date, she didn't do hookups other than virtual ones, and she didn't do anything but work.

The truth was that despite his ridiculously amazing looks, Marcus was probably a safer bet than most.

At least she'd gotten to know him a little through their shared experiences, and he wasn't a total stranger. The man in the adventures had been steadfast and loyal, so there was a good chance that Marcus valued those traits as well.

Besides, what harm could a single meeting do?

If she didn't like him, if they didn't seem compatible, if she decided that she wanted to stick to virtual interactions with him at Perfect Match, then she could tell him that face to face.

And if he refused or caused trouble for her, despite his promise not to, she knew how to handle that.

She wasn't a hapless damsel, and whoever dared to mess with her paid for it dearly. She hadn't earned the nickname 'barracuda' for being a sweetheart.

Marian bit her lower lip and looked at her phone again.

Was she really going to do this?

Was she going to meet the man of her dreams? Who really shouldn't have reached out to her but apparently hadn't been able to help himself because...because he liked her?

Because he wanted to meet the real her?

"Okay, then." Marian picked up her phone and carefully deleted the No.

She typed instead, *Let's do it*, and hit send before she could second-guess herself.

Putting the phone back down, she rolled over to face her pillow and screamed into it to expel the tension.

She'd done it.

Now the ball was in Marcus's court.

But what if she'd waited too long to answer him?

He could be having second thoughts, or perhaps he'd changed his mind entirely, or—

As her phone buzzed with an incoming text, Marian snatched it up and read the message.

It's a date.

48

MARCUS

The coffee shop Marian had chosen for their meeting was cute but not the sort of place Marcus generally associated with downtown Manhattan. It was tucked away on the ground floor of a shopping center between two garishly bright stores and only had a couple of tables available for actual sitting. Most of its customers simply came in, grabbed their drink or food, and left again, off on their next adventure—or, more likely, their corporate office.

For once, Marcus was glad not to be one of them.

His adventure was about to happen right here, right now.

Provided that Marian showed up.

If she was anything like Claudette, Thalesse, Jocelyn, Diana, or Kiera, she would be there. Maybe she would be a little late, but she wouldn't chicken out.

Looking down at the mug cupped between his hands, he pretended to admire the latte art when, in reality, he was forcing himself not to monitor the time or the entrance to the coffee shop.

Instead, he succumbed once more to his nervous introspection.

Marcus closed his eyes and took a deep breath. He had to be prepared for the possibility that she wouldn't come and accept it as Marian's final answer.

He'd broken the rules by contacting her directly, and she would be a fool not to be wary of meeting him, and from what he'd learned about Marian Ferber, she was anything but.

The woman was a successful divorce attorney with a long list of celebrity clientele and had a reputation for dedication to her clients and utter ruthlessness towards their soon-to-be ex-spouses.

The lady was a shark, but so was he.

The question was whether they could swim in the same pond and be happy.

Given how much he'd enjoyed spending time with her in the virtual world, the answer was yes. But if she was significantly different in real life, the answer might be no.

He hadn't found any pictures of her, but the truth was that he hadn't put much effort into it. He'd judged women by their looks for far too long and had learned the hard way that he was going about it all wrong.

As the saying went, repeating the same mistake and expecting different results was the definition of foolishness.

Marcus was done being led by his dumb handle.

This time, he was going to focus on what was inside the package rather than the pretty wrapping paper. He only hoped that Marian's personality matched her avatars' and was willing to compromise on the looks.

Well, he was still a guy, and sexual attraction was at the top of the list of requirements, so he hoped she was at least pleasant to look at, but he was no longer fixated on beauty.

Those days were over, hopefully never to return.

"Excuse me." A soft voice broke him out of his reveries.

Marcus opened his eyes and looked up at the young, curvy woman in a killer navy suit standing next to his table. Bright brown eyes, thick dark hair arranged in a neat chignon, and a heart-shaped face that was adorned with only minimal makeup, she was very attractive, but she was too young to be the one he was waiting for.

He hadn't checked how old Marian was, but the lady standing next to him wasn't even thirty, and that was much too young to achieve the level of success he'd read about.

"Can I help you?" He rose to his feet because he was a gentleman, and she was still standing.

Even in high heels, she barely reached his chin, and when she looked up at him, his dumb handle decided that it liked her.

"I was wondering if this seat is taken." She smiled.

He would have recognized that smile anywhere. Somehow, the Perfect Match people had captured it in all of her avatars.

Maybe his dumb handle wasn't so dumb after all. It had recognized her before he had.

"It is reserved for you." He pulled out the chair and waited for Marian to sit down before holding out his hand.

"Marcus Shurman. Thank you so much for agreeing to meet me."

"Marian Ferber." She smiled again, and his shaft reacted the same way it had before. "But of course, you already know that." She shook his hand, the touch sending a bolt through him.

Marcus laughed a little self-consciously. "Yeah, I do." He sat back down, hoping his suit jacket covered the incriminating evidence. If he wanted to convince her that he wasn't a stalking creep, he'd better pound that idiot into submission. "I know reaching out to you like that was inappropriate. I should have gone through Perfect Match to request a meeting. But I just couldn't stop thinking about you, and when the opportunity presented itself, I just couldn't wait another moment."

"Hmm," Marian said noncommittally. "It was definitely unexpected. I—um." She seemed to be flustered, her hands clasped in front of her as if she was at the principal's office waiting for an admonition.

What could he do to make her comfortable?

"May I get you a coffee?" he offered.

She looked grateful. "Yes! Americano, with a little cream, please."

"You got it." He got back in line and placed the order, then added on one of the sweet treats he recognized in the case. Thus armed, he headed back to their table.

"Oh, I love ginger cake," she said, taking the fork he held out to her.

"I thought you might." They'd had it in one of their experiences, and she'd been over the moon for it then.

The look Marian gave him was a bit solemn. "Marcus, before we go any further, you need to understand. I'm not the same person in the real world that I am when we're at Perfect Match. The experiences allow us to live out our fantasies, but they don't have much to do with who we are in our actual lives." She took a deep breath like she was steeling herself. "In reality, I'm a workaholic divorce attorney who hasn't been on a date in far too long because of what I see relationships lead to. My last vacation doubled as research into a client's spouse hiding assets in the Canary Islands. I eat too much takeout, watch trashy TV to unwind, and want to be a mo—" she cut herself off.

Marcus could infer what she'd been about to say. She wanted to be a mother someday, and if he was the same man he'd been a few months ago, he would have run screaming at this point.

The old Marcus was gone, though. "I get it," he said gently, holding out his hand.

After a moment, she reached out and took it. Her fingers were soft and smooth, her palm warm against his. "I'm not the same person in the experiences as in real life either. My avatar is daring, suave, and exciting, while I basically stare at a computer and crunch numbers all day long."

Marian chuckled. "I'm sure your work is a little more exciting than that."

"It is, but nobody wants to hear about the sexy things I can do with spreadsheets." He waggled his brows, and she laughed again, making his erection re-inflate in an instant.

What was it about her smiles and laughter that triggered such a Pavlovian response from him? Perhaps it was because humor was such a big part of their shared experiences?

It had usually been a precursor to sex, so yeah, that made sense.

Tilting her head, Marian looked at him from under her incredibly long, thick lashes. "So you're not like the guys in *The Wolf of Wall Street*?"

Marcus laughed. "My boss doesn't even allow foul language in the office. She would have crucified anyone who dared one-tenth of one percent of those shenanigans."

Marian let out a mock relieved breath. "Good. I was afraid you might be a wild party guy, while I'm anything but."

"I'm a creature of routine too. I wake up at the same time every morning, get my ass kicked by my personal trainer, go to work, then hit the clubs in the evening. Or I used to," he amended. "I haven't been to a club in months. They bore me now. The people there, what they're looking for…it's fine for them, but it's no longer what I'm after."

Marian's grip on his hand tightened slightly. "What are you after?"

He sighed. "More. If the experiences have taught me anything, it's that my real life sucked. They opened my eyes to just how lonely I was. I don't need to be flying through space or rescuing a beautiful thief from a dangerous weapons dealer to have a good time—" they shared a smile at the reference to their first experience together "—but I do know that I want more meaning in my life than what I had so far. I want to find a real partner." It had taken Marcus a while to come to this realization, but he was confident in it now. "I want to find someone to actually live with, someone who'll navigate the good times and the bad, who I can trust. And…" He shrugged a little helplessly. "Whenever I pictured that person in my mind, it was you."

"Before you discovered my name, you didn't even know what I looked like." Marian tried to pull her hand out of his grip.

"I didn't before, and I didn't after." He let go of her hand. "Your firm's website doesn't have pictures of the partners. But it was you all the same" He reached for her hand again, and when she put it inside his, he gave it a gentle squeeze. "I would really like to take you out on a real date and get to know the real you." He looked into her eyes. "I don't want to scare you off, though. So, if you want to take some time and think about it, that's fine."

"What do you have in mind?"

Marcus wanted to pump his fist in the air. Instead, he looked around the coffee shop. "This is nice, but we can do better. Do you like sushi?"

Her eyes brightened. "I love it."

"Then you are in for a treat. I'll take you to the best-kept secret in town. You haven't had real sushi until you've eaten at Budi's. Are you busy this evening?"

Her smile was soft and tentative but warm enough to send a thrill down Marcus's spine. If he'd had any doubts about being gone on this woman, he now had none.

Marcus had never thought that he could fall in love. He'd never even known that he wanted to, but now he knew, in his heart of hearts, that what he felt was love.

Now all he had to do was convince Marian to give them a chance.

"I'm not busy," she said.

"Excellent." Marcus grinned. "I feel like we are about to embark on a new adventure sans the experience coordinators. Do you think we can do a better job of designing our own scenario?"

Marian returned his grin. "I'm sure we can."

49

MARCUS

Dating had never been easy for Marcus.

His parents had been strict and wanted him to focus on his studies, so he hadn't been allowed to date in high school apart from formal dances.

In college, he'd been part of a frat house that had always thrown parties, and he'd never had to ask anyone for a date. Women had just been around and interested. As soon as he got into his professional life, he'd gone out with a few women on a more formal basis, but it had just felt like too much to do on top of his already punishing workload. In time, his interactions with women had devolved into picking up vacuous beauties at clubs and hooking up with them for one night.

And now...

Now Marcus was finding it surprisingly easy to make time for someone he was genuinely interested in and enjoyed spending time with. It helped that Marian was interested right back and willing to overlook bumps in the road.

"*Sooo*," she drawled on the weekend of their third date, looking outside at the pouring rain. "I think our picnic is a bust."

It definitely was, but Marcus wasn't ready for their time together to be over. The first date, dinner at his favorite sushi place, had been a success, and so was their second date in an Italian restaurant Marian had recommended.

The picnic had been his idea, and he wasn't going to let a little rain get in the way. "What about a home picnic?" he asked quickly. "You're already here, and I've got the food. My apartment is ten minutes away from here."

She looked surprised. "You want me to come to your place?"

Was that too much too soon?

He didn't want to ruin the good thing they were having by rushing things, but they were both adults, and they'd been intimate plenty of times in the virtual world.

It wasn't the same, he was well aware of that, and Marian might need a little more time to feel safe with him, but by the third date she should have gotten over her initial wariness and learned to trust him.

It wasn't that he expected to have sex with her on the third date, but he needed more than the kiss on the cheek he'd gotten after their first two.

Except, if they started kissing, he doubted that it would end with that.

No, it was too soon.

Marcus hadn't failed to notice that Marian was a little

insecure about her looks, so he'd made sure to shower her with compliments. By now, she shouldn't have any doubts about how hot he found her. In fact, he'd been so hard around her that there was no way she wasn't aware of her effect on him.

She probably needed more time, though, and he shouldn't rush her.

Scrambling for a way out of his hasty invitation, he glanced at the back seat of his Bentley. "If you are uncomfortable with coming to my apartment, we can have a backseat picnic."

Wait, wasn't that even worse?

To his great surprise, Marian leaned over and kissed his cheek. "I would love to have a picnic at your place."

Fifteen minutes later, they were sitting on a blanket that he'd spread over his living room floor with a "sounds of nature" soundtrack playing in the background.

"Your place is really nice," Marian said for the third time since they'd gotten there. "Have you lived here long?"

"Nearly a decade." He looked around, trying to see the place through her eyes.

The penthouse was professionally decorated, and he had a cleaning service twice a week, so the place was spotless. It was also cold and impersonal.

He'd never had a knack for decorating, and homey hadn't been the look he was going for when he'd purchased the place ten years ago.

"It needs a woman's touch," he admitted. "It doesn't look like a home."

Marian shrugged. "It's magazine perfect. I would be

afraid to add even a pillow and mess up the decor." She smiled sheepishly. "I'm not good with things like that."

Did it mean that she really liked his place and wasn't just being polite?

"Can you picture yourself living here?"

Her eyes widened. "It's too early to be talking about moving in together."

That hadn't been what he meant, but if he tried to explain, he would just make things worse.

"Yes, indeed." He reached for the wine bottle and popped the cork.

Looking as disconcerted as he felt, Marian opened the basket and started taking out the finger food his chef had prepared for them.

"Wow," Marian said as she pulled a tiny jar of Dijon mustard out of the bottom of the basket. "Are you sure you're not The Doctor? Because it looks like there's more space in there than there should be."

Marcus's inner nerd, beaten into nothingness after his college years, perked up its ears. "You like *Doctor Who?*"

"Eleven is my favorite," she confided with a little smile.

"Mine too."

It was the nicest supper he could remember—talking about the shows they liked and the books they'd read, places they wanted to go, and experiences, the real-life kind, that they wanted to have.

Marcus showed off his collection of Bond novels, and Marian revealed that she'd actually gone out and bought a replica Fabergé egg after their first experience together.

"I couldn't help it," she said with a giggle. "They were so

beautiful, and I had such an incredible time. I wanted to… commemorate it, I guess."

Marcus raised his wine glass to her. "Here's to making good memories."

"In real life and otherwise," she agreed.

50

MARCUS

"Let's go to your place." Marian took Marcus's hand as they left the movie theater.

It was their fifth date in the span of ten days, and they hadn't taken things farther than talking and kissing.

Well, the kissing had been a very recent addition.

After their fourth date, they'd kissed—passionately—but he'd sensed that she wasn't ready yet, and when he'd escorted her to her apartment, she hadn't invited him in, which had proven that he'd been right.

This time, though, Marcus had a feeling that Marian was ready to take the next step.

He wanted to sing hallelujah, but instead, he smiled and leaned in to kiss her cheek. "Of course. We can watch the original version on television."

She gave him a sultry look that said it all.

It got him so hard that he couldn't wait to get to his

penthouse apartment to strip her out of her dress, and started on it in his private elevator.

When the door opened, Marcus dropped the dress on the floor, hoisted Marian into his arms, and carried her to his bedroom.

Her legs wrapped around his waist, she kissed him for all he was worth, while he kneaded her panty-covered ass.

The sexy lace panties and her bra were gone in the next moment, and as he laid her out on his bed, Marcus took a second to admire the lush female spread out before him.

"Gorgeous," he whispered. "Absolutely breathtaking."

She palmed her breasts. "More beautiful than Claudette?"

Marian tweaked her nipples, and Marcus nearly came in his pants.

"Definitely." He smoothed his hand up her leg. "You are real, and I love how soft and feminine you are." He kept trailing his hand up her inner thigh. "You're perfect." He dipped his head and blew air over her sensitive flesh. "My perfect match."

Her breath hitched as he extended his tongue, and when he flicked just the very tip over her clit, she moaned.

"More."

Oh, there was plenty more in store for her.

Marcus had been planning his conquest for the past ten days and had every move mapped out.

By the time he was done with her, Marian would be one hell of a satisfied lady.

"Oh, God," she groaned as he lapped at her clit, and when

he twisted two fingers inside of her, she repeated those exact words three more times.

Oh, yeah. He was going to prove that agent William Kentworth had nothing on Marcus Shurman, and the same was true for all his other avatars.

The real man was better than the fantasy.

Finding the spot inside her that made her arch her back and moan his name, he rubbed it relentlessly, and in mere seconds her legs clamped around his ears, and she climaxed with a shout.

How he hadn't exploded in his pants yet was a miracle, probably attributed to the countless times he'd jerked off during the past ten days thinking about doing what he had just done.

Ignoring his throbbing erection, he kept licking and pumping gently to prolong her pleasure until her tremors subsided.

"*Fuuuuck*," she finally said, stroking one hand through his hair as she lifted his head to look at him. "That was so good." She grinned at him. "Now it's my turn, but you have to undress first. I need to see that body I was fantasizing about each night."

He arched a brow. "Doing what?"

"You know." She reached with her fingers to where his were still pumping gently. "This." She pressed them deeper inside.

"You've been masturbating while thinking about me?"

"What if I have?"

"What were you imagining?" Withdrawing his fingers, he whipped his shirt over his head.

Her eyes widened with pleasure at what she was seeing. "This."

He popped the button on his pants and pulled them down along with his boxer briefs.

Her eyes turned the size of saucers. "I see that the avatars' impressive sizes were not an exaggeration that you requested. They were modeled after you."

He grinned. "When you've got it, flaunt it, right?"

Marcus was joking. He wasn't nearly as well-endowed as Agent Kentworth and definitely not as hung as the merman. He hadn't requested the augmentation and had wondered whether it had been done at Marian's request.

Apparently not.

"Come here." She licked her lips and held out her arms to him.

He moved up her body, spreading her legs with his thighs, until his erection rested just at her entrance, the warmth and wetness of it calling to him like a siren song.

"I've been waiting for this for so long," she murmured before kissing him.

He slid inside her body at the same time as his tongue slid into her mouth, and her nails dug into his back in pleasure.

Marcus had been worried that after the incredible sex they'd had in the experiences, he'd be a disappointment—not big enough, not enough stamina, not enough skill in pleasing a woman. It was hard to live up to a fantasy.

He had no such worries about Marian, though.

He'd known that the real woman would be far superior to the fantasy, and he'd been right.

With her legs wrapped around his back, thrusting slowly and steadily into her, he lifted his head and looked into her warm, brown eyes. "God, you're beautiful." He sped up a little. "You're the most incredible woman I've ever met. Fuck, I love being inside of you like this. You feel amazing." He kept increasing the speed, retreating and surging in with powerful thrusts.

"Oh my God," Marian breathed. "Oh my God, keep—keep going, keep—"

Keep fucking, or keep talking?

Either way, he was happy to oblige. "You're so gorgeous," he went on, making his thrusts into a grind that targeted her clit. "You're gorgeous all the time, but especially when you're with me like this, and I'm making you come. I want to see you come, sweetheart."

"You—you—yes, fuck!" Marian squeezed her eyes shut as her sheath clenched around his shaft, milking him rhythmically. There was no way Marcus could hold off.

His climax exploded out of him, and by the time he was done, he was barely able to hold himself up on his elbows.

"You," she said faintly. "I can't believe that you made me climax two times. That never happened to me outside of virtual experiences. How did you even do that?"

"Bullheaded persistence," he said, leaning in to kiss her again. "And an incredible lover. You are amazing."

"You're going to give me a praise kink."

He laughed. "That wouldn't be so bad, would it?"

"No." She wrapped her arms around him and pulled his weight down onto her, holding on to him even tighter. His erection was slowly softening, but her body still held him, warm and welcoming. "No, it wouldn't be bad at all. In fact, I'm all for it. Tell me more."

"With pleasure, sweetheart."

51

MARCUS

*O*n the seventh date, Marcus met Marian's coworkers and was duly daunted by her secretary, Lila.

She smiled, leaned in, and said very quietly, "If you hurt her, I promise you'll regret it." She lifted her fist and narrowed her eyes in an attempt to look threatening, which looked comical given her angelic face.

"I won't," he said. "I love her. But don't tell anyone. It's a secret."

Lila looked at him for a long moment, then nodded.

"You know, I think I believe you."

On the tenth date, Marcus introduced Marian to his partners, and Marjorie shocked him when she pulled Marian into a tight embrace.

"It's about time someone made an honest man out of you." His boss patted his arm. "Marian is the perfect lady for you."

"She is," Marcus agreed wholeheartedly. "She's my perfect match."

"Oh, that's sweet," Gallagher drawled. "Where did you two lovebirds meet?"

Marcus glanced at Marian, she glanced back at him, and then smiled at Gallagher. "Like everyone else these days, we met online."

ON THEIR ELEVENTH DATE, Marcus broached moving in together.

"I know that we haven't been dating for long, but—"

"Okay." Marian leaned in and planted a kiss on his lips. "My place or yours?"

"It's your choice."

"Yours, then. It's bigger."

He'd been hoping she would say that. Her place was nice, but it was almost an hour's drive from his office, and he hated commuting.

"When?"

"As soon as I find someone to take over my lease."

AFTER THAT, they stopped counting dates out loud, but Marcus still knew it was their eighteenth "date" when Marian sat him down for an important talk.

"What is it?" He took her hand. "Are you having second thoughts about moving in with me?"

"Of course not." She smiled. "But I thought that we

should discuss something first." She took a deep breath. "I've always wanted to be a mother," she confessed. "I know I should have clarified this earlier and checked whether you were on board. I love you, but if you don't want children—"

He put a finger on her lips. "You told me at our first meeting," he reminded her. "Or close enough. And I would love to be a father, as long as it's with you."

A year ago, he wouldn't have imagined ever saying those words, but here he was.

"Oh, Marcus." She tackled him down to the couch. "I love you so much."

On their twenty-second date, Marcus got down on his knee at Marian's favorite little restaurant.

"Marian Ferber, would you marry me?"

It was the most exciting and nerve-wracking thing he'd ever done, and given what he had done as Agent Kentworth, that was saying something.

"Of course, I'll marry you!" she exclaimed.

Their waiter and all the other patrons clapped and cheered.

Best. Experience. Ever.

On their twenty-fourth date, they traveled to spend the weekend with her mother and stepdad, her divorced brother, his fiancée and her two adorable little girls. Her father and his new wife joined them for dinner on the last night, and he'd gotten the man's approval.

. . .

On their thirtieth date, they had dinner with his parents, and his mother cried that her baby boy was finally all grown up.

Apparently, she hadn't considered him an adult unless he was married.

52

MARIAN

"It's fine." Marian rolled her eyes.

"It's crooked." Lila put a hand on her hip and gave her another thorough look over. "Definitely crooked."

Marian huffed with impatience. "It's fine, I'm sure."

"Hold still, let me just—" Lila moved around her back, rearranging her veil so that it fell in an even semi-circle around her head, the bottom of the lace just barely touching the tops of her breasts and her shoulder blades. Then she stepped back and took a long look, satisfaction finally apparent on her face. "Now it's fine." She smirked a little bit. "And so are you, hon. Who would have thought a year ago that you'd end up walking down the aisle toward your very own happily ever after?"

"Not me," Marian confessed, looking at her reflection in the full-length mirror in front of her.

She and Lila were the only ones in the bridal suite—her parents were here, but her mom wasn't the sort to hover, and Marian preferred it that way. Smoothing her hands down her hips, Marian stared at her reflection in the mirror. The dress was a custom mermaid-fitted gown, white satin with pink accent crystals and a jeweled belt that distracted from the little bump of her belly just beneath it.

Not a belly. A baby. Her and Marcus's baby.

Marian pressed her hands to the bump, smoothing over it with her palms as she imagined the child growing inside her. A boy, a girl—they didn't know yet, but whatever it was, Marian couldn't wait to welcome them to the world.

She was going to be a mother and a wife. She wasn't sure which of those felt more improbable to her, given the arc of her life and how she'd been feeling about her chances at either of these outcomes a year ago.

Marian wasn't alone anymore. She was going to have a family with the man she loved, who loved her back and had given her the world.

Marcus. I never saw you coming, but you're everything I needed.

"Aww, you look so in love!" Lila wrapped her arms around Marian from behind and poked her head over her shoulder. "I must admit, I was skeptical when I first met Marcus. I mean, online dating is one thing, but getting into each other's heads the way you did and having all those experiences...it seemed like a setup for disappointment, you know?"

"I know," Marian agreed. "I felt the same way when Marcus first reached out, but I'm so glad he did."

So, so glad.

She couldn't imagine life without him now. Their shared experiences had become the foundation of a real, loving relationship, one that they were about to take to the next level.

Marriage. Her. Incredible.

"All right, enough mushy stuff. You're going to ruin your makeup," Lila groused, discreetly wiping her eyes as she moved in front of Marian again. "Are you ready for this? A Bond-themed wedding, my God." She chuckled. "I can't believe he talked you into this. Your cake is ridiculous, you know that? Cake toppers holding guns!"

"I don't know," Marian said with a grin, "I like them."

"Invitations printed with a picture of you two centered in a gun barrel."

"It's classic."

"A custom martini menu!"

"Don't tell me that you don't like a gin martini, because I know you'd be lying." Marian grinned at her friend. "You'll have to have one for me, all right? Since I'm drinking sparkling apple cider tonight."

"I'll have one for each of you since I know Marcus is teetotaling with you," Lila promised. "All right, then." She handed over Marian's bouquet. "Let's do this. Let's get you married."

Marian nodded firmly. "I'm ready."

53

MARIAN

Marian didn't remember much of her wedding once she got to the church where her husband-to-be and all their friends and family were waiting. Every sense was honed toward Marcus, toward seeing him again. If her father hadn't been there to give her a gentle nudge when the wedding march started, she might have missed her cue entirely. As it was, though, Marian stepped shakily into the aisle and, from the moment she saw Marcus, zeroed in on him like a magnet turning toward true north.

It helped that the moment their eyes met, his widened like he'd been struck, mouth dropping open in awe. He'd looked at her like she was everything to him.

Marian hoped she was because God knew he was everything to her.

She passed rows of guests in a daze. Most of them were smiling, but some were wearing frowns. Several of her closer clients, Gigi included, probably thought they were watching Marian make the worst mistake of her life.

Some of Marcus's coworkers were smirking and rolling their eyes, probably joking about balls and chains.

There were doubters out there. There always were.

She didn't care, though.

All Marian cared about was the moment Marcus reached out and took her hands in his and the look of absolute love on his face when he leaned toward her and whispered, "You look incredible. I'm the luckiest man in the world."

"I'm the luckiest woman," she whispered back before the wedding march ended, and the reverend motioned for people to take their seats.

The sermon was brief, the vows were heartfelt, and the kiss at the end...that was phenomenal. Marian wasn't aware of anyone else once she was in Marcus's arms, held tight as he kissed her breathless.

Only as the wolf whistles and applause finally broke through her reverie did she realize it was done.

They were married.

Married.

"I love you so much." She didn't even realize she was speaking until Marcus leaned in and kissed her again.

"I love you too," he said, just for her ears, before they finally turned to face their guests with broad smiles as they walked back down the aisle as man and wife.

The reception was held in a beautiful mansion offered by Marcus's boss, Marjorie Cage. Apparently, it had been in her family for almost two centuries and had hosted special events for some of New York's most famous and most infamous people over the years.

Even getting through the door was considered an honor, as it housed millions of dollars worth of exquisite art and period pieces. There were bouncers, for crying out loud. Bouncers for protecting furniture, and here Marian was having her reception in the ballroom not twenty feet away from an original Monet.

"Don't worry," Marcus had told her more than once as they toured the place. "She wouldn't have offered it to us if she wasn't comfortable with it. Nobody tells Marjorie what to do."

All their preparations meant that Marian could relax and enjoy the party tonight. And she was more than ready for a party at this point. A delay for pictures with their bridal party meant that she and Marcus were the last to the reception. Their limousine pulled up in front of the mansion, lit and decorated and already ringing with laughter and music, and Marian just sat and stared at it for a long moment.

"Are you all right?" Marcus asked, rubbing his thumb across the back of her hand. "Is Baby acting up?"

Baby had been responsible for more than one bout of morning sickness...or afternoon sickness...or evening sickness, depending on the day. Marcus had been great throughout it all, but Marian was relieved to be able to simply shake her head this time.

"No, I just...." She glanced at him and smiled. "I'm just enjoying one more moment with only the two of us. When we go in there, we'll be in charge of the party. That'll be fun, but I just wanted one more minute that's only about the two of us."

"That's understandable," he said.

He sat back against the seat and pulled Marian into his arms. She nestled in close and shut her eyes, listening to the sound of his heartbeat and savoring what was probably their final moment of intimacy for the night.

"You know, no matter how many people pull on us in there," Marcus said after a moment, "or how much time we have to spend apart, you're the only person I'll be thinking about. No matter where I am or what I'm doing, you're always on my mind. It feels like everything came together really quickly, but I want you to know that I've never had any second thoughts. You're it for me, and I'm so excited that we'll be parents soon." His hand smoothed over her belly. "You've given me a life I didn't even know to hope for, and I can't wait to live it."

"I feel the same," Marian managed once she remembered how to breathe again. "For you. You're the center of my world, you and Baby." She lifted her head for a tender kiss, focusing every nerve she possessed on the man in her arms. "I love you," she said, then kissed him again before pulling away. "And now, Mr. Bond…." Marian grinned devilishly. "Are you ready for a night to remember?"

"Lead on," Marcus replied with a smile. They got out of the limousine and headed for the door of the mansion side by side. As soon as their planner caught sight of them, he fluttered over.

"Everything is going perfectly according to plan. The caterers are standing by, the alcohol is flowing nicely—good call on the martini bar, by the way—and as soon as everyone is done with dinner, we will start in on the dances. But first, your introduction."

They shared a glance. "Let's do it," Marcus said.

"All right, then!" Their planner got on his microphone and opened the double doors leading into the ballroom. "Ladies and gentlemen! Allow me to introduce to you our newlyweds, Marian and Marcus!"

Marian had decided to keep her last name for now, given that it was well-known in professional circles, but their baby would share both names.

Ferber-Shurman was a mouthful, and Marcus joked that it sounded like an accounting firm's name, but it was fine. Maybe Baby would turn out to be an accountant.

They stepped into the tastefully decorated black and white ballroom to fresh applause.

Marian beamed as she caught sight of her former client Veronica and her now-reconciled husband, Oliver. The couple seemed almost as happy as she and Marcus were right now.

Remembering how disappointed she'd been with Veronica when her client announced that she would forgive him, Marian felt guilty.

She'd been so naïve. Love was worth fighting for. Some things couldn't be forgiven, but people certainly could be.

The food was exquisite, catered by Marian's favorite Italian restaurant. The owner, Giacinta, had cried as she brought heaping plates to both of them, congratulating them in Italian and English on their wedding.

"You'll be so happy," she gushed, then glared at Marcus. "You better make this lovely woman happy, *si*?"

"*Si, si,*" he said quickly, making everyone in earshot laugh.

The toasts were better than Marian had expected. Marcus's best man, his friend and trainer Doug, made a heartfelt speech that made everyone laugh as he, not at all modestly, took credit for getting Marcus through the door at Perfect Match.

"Let this be a lesson to you," he said to Marcus, "whenever you're trying to get out of mountain climbing or a marathon—all of my ideas are good!"

"A single data point doesn't make a trend," Marcus shot back.

"Sorry, nobody here thinks math jokes are funny, you nerd."

Lila also gave a speech, which was just as funny if a little more cutting.

"Nobody knows what the future holds," she said, looking at Marian with a gaze that was somewhere between wistful and joyous. "All we can do is put our best effort in and try. You two need to remember that when things get tough, which they will, nothing good comes for free, but if you're in this together, and I think you are, you suck it up and try. And when you try hard enough, well, beautiful things can happen, and wonderful dreams can come true." She lifted her champagne glass. "Here's to two of the most beautiful and wonderful people I know. May all your dreams come true."

Their first dance was to "Nobody Does It Better" from

The Spy Who Loved Me, and they danced late into the night. By the time they made it to the bridal chamber on the second story of the mansion, it was late enough that even Marcus's club-crawling coworkers were planning to head home instead of going back out on the town.

"Oh, my God." Marian kicked off her heels just inside the door with an appreciative groan. "I'm glad we threw an epic party, but damn, I'm exhausted. It felt so long by the end."

"Yeah, it did." Before she knew what was happening, Marian was up in the air, swept off her feet by Marcus, who carried her over to the king-sized bed. She gasped and wrapped her hands around his shoulders. "But I think it went perfectly. And just think," he added as he set her down gently on the edge of the mattress, then knelt in front of her. "We've got three glorious weeks of honeymoon starting tomorrow."

"Mmm, true." Marian watched avidly as Marcus slid his hands up her dress, reaching higher and higher until he found the edge of her thigh-high stockings. "Where I hope to wear a lot less than this most of the time."

"I hope so too," he said, pressing a kiss to her knee as he unclasped the garter belt and began to pull the stockings down. "Personally, my preference is nude."

Marian laughed. "So I can show off my little belly to the world?"

"Not to the world. Just to me," he said, moving on to her second stocking. His gaze was hot, and his fingers firm as they undressed her. Marian rubbed her thighs together, her mouth dropping open as her pussy began to get wet. "I love looking at every part of you."

"Oh...you, ah." She gasped as he pushed her skirt up until it was gathered around her waist, baring her tiny satin panties to him. He stroked a finger over the slippery material before dipping it inside.

"Mm, me," Marcus agreed, looking at her hungrily. "But I don't think looking is enough tonight, sweetheart. I want to taste you too."

He waited, though—waited for her to tell him it was fine. If she was too tired, if she just wanted to go to bed, he would be fine.

Marian felt a second wind coming on. "I'm all yours," she said, meaning every word.

All yours. Forever, no matter what we're experiencing together.

She wasn't afraid of the future anymore. She had Marcus, they had Baby to look forward to...

And Perfect Match to go back to if they needed an escape.

What a Perfect Match, indeed.

Ready for the next Perfect Match?
MY MERMAN PRINCE

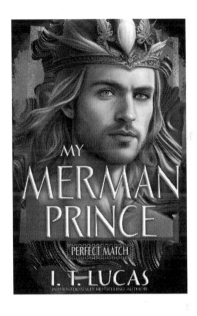

THE BEAUTIFUL ARCHITECT working late on the twelfth floor of my building thinks that I'm just the maintenance guy. She's also under the impression that I'm not interested.

Nothing could be further from the truth.

I want her like I've never wanted a woman before, but I don't play where I work.

I don't need the complications.

When she tells me about living out her mermaid fantasy with a stranger in a Perfect Match virtual adventure, I decide to do everything possible to ensure that the stranger is me.

Dear reader,

Thank you for reading Perfect Match: The Thief Who Loved Me. As an independent author, I rely on your support to spread the word. If you enjoyed the story, I would be grateful if you could post a brief review on Amazon.

Kind words will be greatly appreciated and get good Karma sent your way -:)

Love & happy reading,

Isabell

Also by I. T. Lucas

PERFECT MATCH
Vampire's Consort
King's Chosen
Captain's Conquest
The Thief Who Loved Me
My Merman Prince

THE CHILDREN OF THE GODS ORIGINS
1: Goddess's Choice
2: Goddess's Hope

THE CHILDREN OF THE GODS

Dark Stranger
1: Dark Stranger The Dream
2: Dark Stranger Revealed
3: Dark Stranger Immortal

Dark Enemy
4: Dark Enemy Taken
5: Dark Enemy Captive
6: Dark Enemy Redeemed

Kri & Michael's Story
6.5: My Dark Amazon

Dark Warrior
7: Dark Warrior Mine
8: Dark Warrior's Promise

ALSO BY I. T. LUCAS

9: Dark Warrior's Destiny
10: Dark Warrior's Legacy

Dark Guardian

11: Dark Guardian Found
12: Dark Guardian Craved
13: Dark Guardian's Mate

Dark Angel

14: Dark Angel's Obsession
15: Dark Angel's Seduction
16: Dark Angel's Surrender

Dark Operative

17: Dark Operative: A Shadow of Death
18: Dark Operative: A Glimmer of Hope
19: Dark Operative: The Dawn of Love

Dark Survivor

20: Dark Survivor Awakened
21: Dark Survivor Echoes of Love
22: Dark Survivor Reunited

Dark Widow

23: Dark Widow's Secret
24: Dark Widow's Curse
25: Dark Widow's Blessing

Dark Dream

26: Dark Dream's Temptation
27: Dark Dream's Unraveling
28: Dark Dream's Trap

Dark Prince

29: Dark Prince's Enigma
30: Dark Prince's Dilemma

ALSO BY I. T. LUCAS

31: DARK PRINCE'S AGENDA

DARK QUEEN

32: DARK QUEEN'S QUEST

33: DARK QUEEN'S KNIGHT

34: DARK QUEEN'S ARMY

DARK SPY

35: DARK SPY CONSCRIPTED

36: DARK SPY'S MISSION

37: DARK SPY'S RESOLUTION

DARK OVERLORD

38: DARK OVERLORD NEW HORIZON

39: DARK OVERLORD'S WIFE

40: DARK OVERLORD'S CLAN

DARK CHOICES

41: DARK CHOICES THE QUANDARY

42: DARK CHOICES PARADIGM SHIFT

43: DARK CHOICES THE ACCORD

DARK SECRETS

44: DARK SECRETS RESURGENCE

45: DARK SECRETS UNVEILED

46: DARK SECRETS ABSOLVED

DARK HAVEN

47: DARK HAVEN ILLUSION

48: DARK HAVEN UNMASKED

49: DARK HAVEN FOUND

DARK POWER

50: DARK POWER UNTAMED

51: DARK POWER UNLEASHED

52: DARK POWER CONVERGENCE

ALSO BY I. T. LUCAS

DARK MEMORIES
53: DARK MEMORIES SUBMERGED
54: DARK MEMORIES EMERGE
55: DARK MEMORIES RESTORED

DARK HUNTER
56: DARK HUNTER'S QUERY
57: DARK HUNTER'S PREY
58: DARK HUNTER'S BOON

DARK GOD
59: DARK GOD'S AVATAR
60: DARK GOD'S REVIVISCENCE
61: DARK GOD DESTINIES CONVERGE

DARK WHISPERS
62: DARK WHISPERS FROM THE PAST
63: DARK WHISPERS FROM AFAR
64: DARK WHISPERS FROM BEYOND

DARK GAMBIT
65: DARK GAMBIT THE PAWN
66: DARK GAMBIT THE PLAY
67: DARK GAMBIT RELIANCE

DARK ALLIANCE
68: DARK ALLIANCE KINDRED SOULS
69: DARK ALLIANCE TURBULENT WATERS
70: DARK ALLIANCE PERFECT STORM

DARK HEALING
71: DARK HEALING BLIND JUSTICE
72: DARK HEALING BLIND TRUST

ALSO BY I. T. LUCAS

THE CHILDREN OF THE GODS SERIES SETS

BOOKS 1-3: DARK STRANGER TRILOGY—INCLUDES A BONUS SHORT STORY: **THE FATES TAKE A VACATION**

BOOKS 4-6: DARK ENEMY TRILOGY —INCLUDES A BONUS SHORT STORY—**THE FATES' POST-WEDDING CELEBRATION**

BOOKS 7-10: DARK WARRIOR TETRALOGY
BOOKS 11-13: DARK GUARDIAN TRILOGY
BOOKS 14-16: DARK ANGEL TRILOGY
BOOKS 17-19: DARK OPERATIVE TRILOGY
BOOKS 20-22: DARK SURVIVOR TRILOGY
BOOKS 23-25: DARK WIDOW TRILOGY
BOOKS 26-28: DARK DREAM TRILOGY
BOOKS 29-31: DARK PRINCE TRILOGY
BOOKS 32-34: DARK QUEEN TRILOGY
BOOKS 35-37: DARK SPY TRILOGY
BOOKS 38-40: DARK OVERLORD TRILOGY
BOOKS 41-43: DARK CHOICES TRILOGY
BOOKS 44-46: DARK SECRETS TRILOGY
BOOKS 47-49: DARK HAVEN TRILOGY
BOOKS 50-52: DARK POWER TRILOGY
BOOKS 53-55: DARK MEMORIES TRILOGY
BOOKS 56-58: DARK HUNTER TRILOGY
BOOKS 59-61: DARK GOD TRILOGY
BOOKS 62-64: DARK WHISPERS TRILOGY
BOOKS 65-67: DARK GAMBIT TRILOGY

MEGA SETS

INCLUDE CHARACTER LISTS

ALSO BY I. T. LUCAS

THE CHILDREN OF THE GODS: BOOKS 1-6
THE CHILDREN OF THE GODS: BOOKS 6.5-10

TRY THE CHILDREN OF THE GODS SERIES ON AUDIBLE

2 FREE audiobooks with your new Audible subscription!

THE PERFECT MATCH SERIES

Perfect Match: Vampire's Consort

When Gabriel's company is ready to start beta testing, he invites his old crush to inspect its medical safety protocol.

Curious about the revolutionary technology of the *Perfect Match Virtual Fantasy-Fulfillment studios*, Brenna agrees.

Neither expects to end up partnering for its first fully immersive test run.

Perfect Match: King's Chosen

When Lisa's nutty friends get her a gift certificate to *Perfect Match Virtual Fantasy Studios*, she has no intentions of using it. But since the only way to get a refund is if no partner can be found for her, she makes sure to request a fantasy so girly and over the top that no sane guy will pick it up.

Except, someone does.

Warning: This fantasy contains a hot, domineering crown prince, sweet insta-love, steamy love scenes painted with light shades of gray, a wedding, and a HEA in both the virtual and real worlds.

Intended for mature audience.

Perfect Match: Captain's Conquest

Working as a Starbucks barista, Alicia fends off flirting all day long, but none of the guys are as charming and sexy as Gregg. His frequent visits are the highlight of her day, but since he's never asked her out, she assumes he's taken. Besides, between a day job and a budding music career, she has no time to start a new relationship.

That is until Gregg makes her an offer she can't refuse—a gift certificate to the virtual fantasy fulfillment service everyone is talking about. As a huge Star Trek fan, Alicia has a perfect match in mind—the captain of the Starship Enterprise.

The Thief Who Loved Me

When Marian splurges on a Perfect Match Virtual adventure as a world infamous jewel thief, she expects high-wire fun with a hot partner who she will never have to see again in real life.

A virtual encounter seems like the perfect answer to Marcus's string of dating disasters. No strings attached, no drama, and definitely no love. As a die-hard James Bond fan, he chooses as his avatar a dashing MI6 operative, and to complement his adventure, a dangerously seductive partner.

Neither expects to find their forever Perfect Match.

My Merman Prince

The beautiful architect working late on the twelfth floor of my building thinks that I'm just the maintenance guy. She's also under the impression that I'm not interested.

Nothing could be further from the truth.

I want her like I've never wanted a woman before, but I don't play where I work.

I don't need the complications.

When she tells me about living out her mermaid fantasy with a stranger in a Perfect Match virtual adventure, I decide to do everything possible to ensure that the stranger is me.

FOR EXCLUSIVE PEEKS

FOR EXCLUSIVE PEEKS AT UPCOMING RELEASES & A FREE COMPANION BOOK

Join my *VIP Club* and gain access to the VIP portal at itlucas.com
click here to join

INCLUDED IN YOUR FREE MEMBERSHIP:

YOUR VIP PORTAL

- Read preview chapters of upcoming releases.
- Listen to Goddess's Choice narration by C. Lawrence
- Exclusive content offered only to my VIPs.

FREE I.T. LUCAS COMPANION INCLUDES:

FOR EXCLUSIVE PEEKS

- GODDESS'S CHOICE PART 1
- PERFECT MATCH: VAMPIRE'S CONSORT
- INTERVIEW Q & A
- CHARACTER CHARTS

IF YOU'RE ALREADY A SUBSCRIBER, YOU'LL RECEIVE A DOWNLOAD LINK FOR MY NEXT BOOK'S PREVIEW CHAPTERS IN THE NEW RELEASE ANNOUNCEMENT EMAIL. IF YOU ARE NOT GETTING MY EMAILS, YOUR PROVIDER IS SENDING THEM TO YOUR JUNK FOLDER, AND YOU ARE MISSING OUT ON **IMPORTANT UPDATES, SIDE CHARACTERS' PORTRAITS, ADDITIONAL CONTENT, AND OTHER GOODIES.** TO FIX THAT, ADD isabell@itlucas.com TO YOUR EMAIL CONTACTS OR YOUR EMAIL VIP LIST.

Perfect Match: The Thief Who Loved Me is a work of fiction! Names, characters, places and incidents are products of the author's imagination or are used fictitiously and are not to be construed as real. Any similarity to actual persons, organizations and/or events is purely coincidental.

Copyright © 2023 by I. T. Lucas

All rights reserved.

No part of this book may be reproduced in any form or by any electronic or mechanical means, including information storage and retrieval systems, without written permission from the author, except for the use of brief quotations in a book review.

Published by Evening Star Press

EveningStarPress.com

ISBN: 978-1-957139-66-1

Made in United States
Orlando, FL
31 August 2023

36588430R00167